© ANDREA JOLIAT

**Andrew Goldstein** is in the third act of his adult life. Act I: Husband, writer, tree planter, assistant librarian, organic orange and olive farmer, school bus driver, Zamboni driver, editor, tennis pro, stock broker, power transformer tube winder. Act II: Father, no longer writer, custom builder, youth soccer coach. Act III: Grandfather, table tennis player, writer again, lives in Concord, Massachusetts and enjoys waking up each morning to the birds chirping and the day that awaits him. *The Bookie's Son* is his first novel.

# THE BOOKIE'S SON

ANDREW GOLDSTEIN

(sixoneseven)BOOKS

Boston

## Other 617 books

*Annie Begins* by Michelle Toth
"A winning debut—a moving and engaging novel that will have you rooting for Annie from page one."

—Jennifer Sturman, author of the *Rachel Benjamin and Delia Truesdale series*

*Veronica's Nap* by Sharon Bially
"*Veronica's Nap* is such a compelling story I read it in one sitting. Sharon Bially speaks with eloquence to the hopes, the dreams and fears that we all share but often dare not express."

—Han Nolan, National Book Award-winning author of *Dancing on the Edge*

*Twelve Weeks* by Karen Lee Sobol
"Karen Lee Sobol, an accomplished artist, describes her journey through treatment for a rare life-threatening blood disease with eloquence, wit, and occasional tears...Karen Lee's narrative is warm, insightful, inspirational, and skillfully illustrated with her own artwork."

—Marvin J. Stone, MD, Baylor Sammons Cancer Center

Printed in the United States of America.

ISBN: 978-0-9848245-0-2

*for my mother and father and grandmother*

# The Bookie's Son

# SUMMER, 1960: THE BRONX

# 1.

The day started uneventfully. I was just a boy then, fighting in my parents' bedroom against imaginary foes. I ran to the bathroom and pulled my grandmother's false teeth out of a glass of water on the sink. Then I darted back and set the teeth in the crease of a large pillow leaning against the quilted headboard of the king-sized bed. Like a ventriloquist controlling a puppet, I moved the teeth up and down and said in a squeaky voice, "You might as well forget it, squirt. You're covered from all sides. Just drop the knife and maybe you'll live, right boys?"

The telephone ringing sounded like a siren signaling danger, a call to arms to help the only man brave enough to...fat chance, the spell was broken. I slammed my fist into the pillow and sent the teeth diving on to the mattress. I picked up the telephone on the fifth ring.

"Hello," I answered, groggily.

"Hi, Ricky, this is Frankie."

"Hello Frankie." I had met him a couple of times. He was in his forties, with a big belly, and pimples like a teenager.

"You studying for your Bar Mitzvah like a good boy?"

"My Hebrew book is right in front of me." I slid the book along the floor with my toes.

"This is all at Yonkers. Six dollars on Jeremy's Gal in the fourth. Ten dollars on Donovan's Daughter in the seventh."

"Playing the young ladies tonight, Frankie?"

"Right. Four dollars on—"

"Hello, hello," Rosie, my grandmother, shouted into another of the five phones in our small apartment.

"Grandma, I got it."

"Hello, hello, who is this?" she persisted.

"Frankie."

"Grandma, I've—"

"Ricky? Ricky? Where are you?"

"Grandma, it's business," I said severely. This scene repeated itself every day with only minor variations. When my father developed his ulcer he blamed it on Rosie. Now I knew why.

"Hankie, you wanna bet the horses? Let's go partners. Ha ha…"

"Grandma, hang up!"

"I'll hang up when I want!" She stamped her foot loud enough for me to hear in stereo.

"Grandma, hang up now!"

She slammed the phone down.

I took two more bets from Frankie before I hopped off the bed, returned Grandma's teeth to the bathroom, and went to find her. She lived in our Bronx apartment during the week, cooking and cleaning and watching after me, while my parents worked in Manhattan. On the weekends she went to her own apartment near Yankee Stadium to be with her boyfriend, ninety-year-old Mr. Fein. Though she had been dating him for twenty years she still called him by his last name. They never married because he had an unmarried daughter who still lived with him.

When I entered the kitchen, Grandma was standing at the stove. She was almost blind and nearly deaf and had shrunk to just over five feet. Beneath her housedress, her schmatte as she called it, her large breasts hung down to her belly. She blew into the boiling chicken broth and stirred it with a wooden ladle. She once bragged to me that she was not only a great cook, but also a great stirrer.

Our kitchen was tiny. If I stood in the center I could pivot and touch the gas stove, refrigerator, sink, cabinets, and red Formica table, all without taking a step. The table served as both a place to eat and as a kitchen counter. The small refrigerator looked like a jukebox.

"I'm going out soon," I said. "Don't take any bets."

"You're not my boss," Grandma said. With her bare hand she pulled a chicken breast out of the boiling broth. This feat never ceased to amaze me.

"Daddy said you're not allowed to take bets. Especially on napkins."

"Daddy said, Daddy said, feh." She turned away and spit. "You want some Jell-O?"

"I'm not hungry."

"I thought you like my Jell-O." She opened the refrigerator and peered into the dimly lit interior.

"I love it. I'm just not hungry."

She held a blue cup in front of my nose as if the smell of black cherry Jell-O was intoxicating. "Have a little. I made it especially for you."

I sat down to eat a little of her fabulous Jell-O. She left the kitchen to fetch her teeth.

When she returned, she shuffled over to the table and put three pennies into the pishkah, a small white metal can with Hebrew letters on it—a charity box that she religiously fed money into. She lectured me often that no matter how poor you were there was always someone in worse shape and that God wanted you to help them. "You're a good boy," she said, sitting down, "but don't be like your father. He's a common man who doesn't know how to treat people."

"I thought I told you not to say bad things about him anymore."

"You're my boss? A little kotchka mocha, you're going to tell me what to do? I can say what I want. He's a shmendrik. He has no sense. No judgment."

"I'll tell Mommy when she comes home from work."

"I'm afraid of her? Ha ha, big deal, Pearl. You see what time she went to bed last night? Two o'clock. Every night. Why doesn't she go to bed early? She works so hard and that bum loses all her money."

She spit her venom onto the table. I looked at her sagging arms. Her skin was tough as cheap leather, but soft as cream between the cracks. The smell and feel of her cast a spell over me. Even when she was being a pain in the ass, there was something about her passion, her emotions rooted to another continent, which made me want to sit with her, talk with her, and stroke her arms. Her love, like the rest of her emotions, was never constrained, never hidden. She loved me full throttle and the warmth of that love filled me with pleasure.

"I knew he was bad. I always could judge people. That's why everyone likes me. They know Rosie Simon knows people. Wherever I go this is what they tell me. I don't make it up."

"You make it up, don't you Grandma?" I teased.

She pounded her palm against her chest. "I swear on my life. They tell me, 'why are you so different? What makes you so smart?'"

I thought about teasing her again. I liked playing with her vanity, but I heard my father unlocking the front door.

"Any bets?" he asked, as he entered the kitchen. He was six-foot-two, quick and wiry. His arms didn't bulge like a weightlifter's, but when you shook his hand or pushed against his broad shoulders, you had an instant awareness of brute strength. A handsome man with green eyes and dimples, but there was something rough about him, coarse and undeveloped. Some people said I looked like him, but my eyes were blue and I was skinnier.

"Only Frankie called."

"You want some chicken?" Grandma asked him.

"I have to go out again."

He was playing hooky from work to make some collections for Nathan Glucksman, a Bronx gangster. My mother had told me that he was feeling blue because he didn't like being an enforcer and that I should cheer him up. So when he went back out, I tagged along.

We walked sluggishly through the humid dark hallway. When we reached the elevator, I stepped inside by myself, turned around, and smiled. No words were spoken, but I saw the spark of agreement. My father, always competitive, immediately switched into a ready position and I pressed the button for the lobby. As the elevator door started to close, Harry Davis was off and running.

By the time the elevator began to descend the four stories, I heard him pounding down the stairs. I pushed my weight to the floor hoping to speed up the elevator's fall. When the door slid open in the lobby I didn't see him. I was thrilled for half a second—maybe I'd finally won but almost simultaneously I wondered why I couldn't hear his footsteps on the concrete treads.

"What took you so long?" he said. He sat on a ratty old lobby chair, winded and wiping sweat off his face with a handkerchief.

As we walked outside on this hot June day Fat Bertha nodded hello from her third-floor window perch across the street. The neighborhood was her beat. You could get in trouble a block away, where there were bullies and gangs and Tony Goostaldi, a weird guy who was worth taking long cuts to avoid. You also had to be careful in the alleys behind the buildings because they were hidden from Fat Bertha. But on the sidewalk, in the neighborhood, you were safe. Fat Bertha was always there, protecting everyone, from sunrise till past midnight. In the morning when I looked out my window, she was staring at me. On the sidewalk, from first base (the fire hydrant) or second (the sewer manhole), whenever I looked up, she was watching. She was like one of those portrait paintings that no matter what angle you looked at it from, the eyes were always on you. She saw everything and knew everything that went on in the neighborhood.

My father and I waved to her. Old people sat gossiping on beach chairs lined up next to the curb. Above them the Jerome Avenue elevated train tracks hovered like a prehistoric centipede. My friends were playing punch-ball on the wide sidewalk. They shouted hello to both of us. Harry was the only father who sometimes played ball games with them. His mammoth home runs were legendary.

A pink Spaldeen rubber ball, about the size of a tennis ball—the ball of choice in the Bronx, 1960, for stickball, punch-ball, box-ball, and off-the-stoop—came bouncing over the heads of the old people. They screamed curses at my friends in English and Yiddish and Italian.

My father and I walked up to the Grand Concourse, a wide boulevard with eleven lanes of moving traffic flanked by broad concrete sidewalks, multi-story brick buildings, stores, and trees. The sidewalks were filled with people, old, young, mostly white. Shirtless hairy men sat on stoops. Ladies wearing loose-fitting schmattes wheeled shopping carts stolen from the Daitch Shopwell. Trapped heat radiated from the bricks and concrete, but I could feel in the breeze and see in the darkening sky that relief was on the way. My father picked up the pace. He gave me a dollar to go to Jahn's ice cream parlor and wait for him while he made his collections.

Big storm clouds, black and thick, snuffed out the available light. The thunder sounded like it was still far away, but the rain came with no warning drizzle. It was an instant deluge. The Fordham Road sewers overflowed and people scattered under wet awnings. Too late to go to Jahn's I ran with my father into the tailor shop.

"Excuse me," he said, walking toward the counter. "Excuse me!" The tailor's head lay in his folded arms.

"What time is it?" The tailor reached for his glasses. "It's so dark. You're all wet."

My father glanced at his watch, but he didn't volunteer the time. Two fluorescent light fixtures hung from the low ceiling, humming.

"So...what can I do for you?" The tailor squinted as he put on his glasses. I noticed the blue numbers on his hairless arm. "Come closer," he said. He waved a tiny hand at me. I stepped toward him. My father didn't budge.

"You owe some money," my father said.

"I owe a lot of money...to many people." The tailor's voice tightened.

"You owe over two thousand dollars to Nathan Glucksman."

"Yes, this is true, but fifteen hundred is interest."

"That doesn't concern me." My father's hands closed into fists. "I've come to collect what you owe him."

I cringed. The few times that I had accompanied my father on the collections he had always sent me to Jahn's or Alexander's to buy something. I knew what went on inside the stores but I had never before seen it or heard it. Looking at the fear in the tailor's face, I didn't want to be there. I could tell my father didn't want me there either, the way he kept glancing out the window, but the storefront glass was being pelted with waves of windblown rain.

"Believe me, if I had it, I would give him long ago. Three months ago the others came. The Spratz brothers. They wrecked my shop. Was this smart? Now it will take me longer to pay him back."

I kept staring at the tailor, trying not to focus on the etchings on his arm. Like my father I was good with numbers, and without meaning to I started adding them up, as if that would give me insight into the tailor. I would know his sum.

The tailor looked at me but addressed my father. "If you don't mind me asking, are you Jewish?"

"How can you tell?" My father tapped on his crooked nose, broken several times while boxing.

The tailor, shyly smiling, leaned toward us. "You know I have mixed feelings," he said. His eyes focused on my father's clenched fists. "I hate that goniff Glucksman. This is what the Germans did. They took the Jews and made them punish other Jews. On the other hand, it's nice to see a big strong Jewish man. If we had more of those. Jewish muscle."

My father had been a boxing champion in the Army. He radiated power. "I want the money," he said as he stepped around the counter and walked closer to the tailor.

The tailor shifted his stare back to me. His brown eyes looked dark and sad. "Put on some weight," he said kindly. "Be strong like your father."

"I eat a lot of Jell-O. My grandmother tells me it's good for the bones." I hoped he couldn't look into my brain to see all the fights I had chickened out of, all the bullies I'd run away from. I was a thin, anemic twelve-year-old kid.

The tailor smiled, but his voice cracked as he spoke to my father. "So what's it going to be, Mr. Jewish Gangster and good father? A leg? An arm? You going to take out my eye and give it to your boy?"

"How much can you give me?" My father stepped closer,

standing right over the tailor now.

"Nothing. I wish I could. I'm not a very lucky man, but I like the horses. Why don't you pull up that chair? Your boy, he can sit here on the table."

He pushed a pair of gray pants away from the sewing machine to make room. My father looked angry and I watched nervously, knowing he was capable of anything. I didn't want him to hurt the tailor, but I had felt the fury of his hands and belt many times and those memories froze me into silence.

For a moment, the only sounds in the tailor shop were the humming of the lights and the beating of the rain on the sidewalk, the awning, the glass. The tailor stared at me. My father held his fists still.

But when his hands moved again, they moved quickly, grabbing the tailor by his white shirt and lifting him up in one quick jerk so that he and the tailor were now face to face. "I don't give a fuck about your luck. I want some money."

"Dad!" I screamed.

Lifting the tailor higher, above his head, he turned toward me and said, "You shut up!"

I shook my head and backed away. I blinked my eyes rapidly. He shoved the tailor against the wall, but then lightning lit up the sky and almost instantaneously a tremendous boom shook the plate glass.

My father stood there silently, his eyes darting from the numbers on the tailor's arm to the window. He looked confused. I took a chance. "Dad, that lightening was close," I said.

He lowered the tailor back into his chair.

"You new at this?" The tailor asked. His hands and arms trembled.

"I owe Glucksman money. This is how I'm paying some of it off."

The tailor shook his head. "That goniff—a real Nazi."

My father moved away and grabbed the torn cane chair by the window. "You have to give me something." He looked exhausted as he plopped into the chair.

"I don't have," the tailor said. "What's your name?"

"Harry."

"Harry what?"

"Harry Davis."

"Harry Davis, I'm Morris Marinsky. What kind of work do you do?"

"I work in the garment center. I cut ladies dresses. A little bookmaking and a little this, a little that, on the side."

"You cut, I sew. We both like the horses. And your name?" He turned toward me and stood, offering his hand to shake.

"I'm Ricky Davis."

"Ricky, it's a pleasure."

He stared at me for a long time, clutching my hand with both of his. He wasn't hurting me, just holding on. I felt the tremors in his hands and gave them a slight squeeze, not wanting my father to see. The tailor opened and shut his eyes three times, as if it was a code.

"It doesn't look good if I don't get some money," my father said. "I don't want to have to hurt you."

"I know you don't." Morris let me go and with his hand offered me the sewing table to sit down on. "You're a good father. I wish I could help you. But I can't. Believe me, I understand how hard this is for you, and I'm thankful it's you and not those bulvans he sent last time, but please, break my leg, beat me up, but don't wreck my store. I have to make a living. If you could not harm my hands I would be most grateful."

"Fuck Glucksman," my father said. He paused for a few seconds. Then he clapped his hands and said, "Fuck Glucksman, the hell with him."

"Harry, don't be a hero," Morris said. "What will happen to you when they find out?"

He looked away, out the storefront again. "Maybe I'll have raised the money I owe by then. I have a couple of deals going. I'll figure out something."

"No, no, I can't let you do this." Morris reached over and clasped my father's forearm. Held it for a couple of seconds and then raised it in the air. "Come on, don't make me hurt you." He closed his small hands into tiny fists and punched himself lightly in his face. "Like this Harry, beat me up a little. A few punches, maybe break my nose, so I'll look like you."

My father's lips hinted at a smile. Morris started shadow boxing. He threw some soft punches at my father and then danced around his sewing machine, bringing me into the mix, tossing a few light punches at me. I jumped off the table and bobbed and weaved, movements my father had taught me.

My father laughed out loud, something he seldom did. I laughed too, wanting to share the moment, wanting him to share my affection for the tailor. I wondered if the fact that Morris was a Holocaust survivor made my father feel guilty or confused about what to do. He had been there during the war, liberating the emaciated survivors. He didn't like to talk about it. I knew from past stories that he was still pissed off because the Army transferred him to Europe from China, where he had been stationed in Tientsin, making the most money he had made in his life, "in the sweetest deal ever." According to my mom, all of his prior pool hustling, petty thefts, and scams were small change compared to China.

Or maybe he was giving Morris a break and acting nice to him because I was there? Or was this the "bad judgment" my mother always spoke about?

"Ahhhh, I would have been better off with the goons," Morris said. He took a screwdriver from a drawer in the sewing table. He walked to the back of the store and bent down. Using the tool as a lever, he pulled up two floorboards. Breathing heavily through his nose, he lifted an ancient wooden box that looked like an antique music box. When he opened it I smelled camphor.

Morris handed the box to my father. "Here, take it. There's over eight hundred dollars. I was saving to go to Israel. I figured with two thousand I could start a new life."

My father looked down at the box. The numbers tattooed on Morris's arm drew my eyes again. Whether or not my father noticed them or they influenced him, he didn't say, but he pushed the box away as he rose from his chair. "Get out of here."

"Take it, take it, I'm an old man. Please. I have no children. You have a son. A future."

"How could you go to Israel? What about the shop? You have a buyer?"

"What's there to buy? I take my sewing machine with me and there's no shop. Now I'm a tailor in Israel."

I looked around the small store. Except for the rumpled clothes stacked on the counter and the sewing table, there was nothing of value.

I glanced out the window. The sky was clearing. The storm

had passed and the shoppers were out again. I hopped off the table and walked over to the window to see if there was a rainbow.

We were three men in a room, waiting for something to happen. It felt good—like when I was among the gamblers talking horses in Joe's candy store or in our apartment with the gin players shrouded in a smoky haze—even if I was just a shadow.

Morris tried to give the money to my father again, and again my father pushed it away. Morris gave in and thanked my father, who nodded and looked at me and then at Morris and then at me before he reached into his pocket for his wallet. He counted out the collections he had made in the morning, almost six hundred dollars. He kept a twenty and put the rest in Morris's wooden box.

"Don't wait for two thousand, you've got enough. Buy a ticket tomorrow and leave. It's better for both of us."

Morris couldn't take his eyes off the money. His body swayed forward and backward. "Except for my niece I have no family. My wife and six children were killed by the Nazis. My youngest, Miriam, was nine months old, and they crushed her like a plastic doll before my eyes. For seventeen years I've stitched and played the horses, not allowing, forgetting... Now a stranger comes into my shop. Mr. Jewish Gangster, Mr. Harry Davis."

I brushed my forehead with my palm, pretending to wipe away sweat across my eyes as I blotted my tears. Neither my father nor Morris was crying. I looked away from them, hoping they didn't see the wetness.

"Here's my address," my father said, writing it down.

"Send us a postcard from Israel."

"Harry, why are you doing this for me?"

"It's not for you. I'm doing it for my son, so he knows right from wrong. Knows how to be a good man. A mensch."

Morris gripped the box hard. "What will happen to you?"

"Maybe a horse will come in," my father said.

"A dark horse."

## 2.

"Your father is an idiot," my mother said. She was sitting opposite me at the kitchen table as I told her about my afternoon adventure in the tailor shop. She was still dressed in her work clothes, a brown skirt and tan blouse, a double-strand gold-colored necklace, and rhinestone earrings. In her teens she had wanted to become a movie star—she was smart and beautiful, thick black hair, dark skin, brown eyes that looked black in most light, high cheekbones, and emotion that oozed out of her—but she married young and after my sister, Suzy, was born and my father went overseas during World War II, she got a job as a secretary to a talent agent. She told me that she was the one who discovered Harry Belafonte, though her boss took the credit. She switched jobs in 1957, when I was 10-years-old, and became the private secretary to Arthur Posner, the top theatrical lawyer in New York.

He was cheap with his employees, but generous in other ways. He gave my mother power and prestige. Though she was only a secretary with a tenth-grade education, she read and approved scripts, controlled house seats at sold-out Broadway shows, and had access to the stars her boss represented. Difficult clients like Orson Welles and Otto Preminger trusted only Pearl Davis to review their documents. She attended theatrical openings and the Tony awards, and whenever she wanted she could call for free limousine rides in return for all the business she gave the limousine company. While these perks didn't build her bank account, they seemed to fill some of the hollows in her life and buoy her up when she was overcome with a sense of failure.

She kept shaking her head as I told her more details about the exchange between Morris and my father. Chatter from people on the street corner, and the rumble of trains going by on the elevated tracks, streamed through the open window behind her.

"But Mom, the tailor was a really nice man and his children were murdered during the war."

"He always has to be a big shot," she said, hunched over, "impress the waitresses, the sales clerks. What about us?"

"Daddy said he's working on a deal. He'll get the money before Nathan knows."

"Nathan will kill him if he finds out."

"I thought he was your friend."

"You know, you're as stupid as your father." She leaned her face closer to me, as if her black-eyed stare wasn't intimidating enough. "That tailor is a stranger. I don't care how nice he is. He's a stranger. I'm his wife. What about me? When Nathan finds out your father gave away his money do you think he'll care that the tailor's children were murdered? A big shot with strangers. When do I get that treatment?"

Tears streaked down her cheeks. I wiped them away with my hand.

"Shit!" she said. "Why couldn't we catch a break? Just once."

"Daddy was only…"

"Bad judgment." That was her code for my father's history of reckless decisions that usually left us broke. The fireproof pajamas, the Studebaker stock, the land deal in Cuba, were past money-making schemes that had backfired. Now his most recent sure thing—the smuggled tax-free cigarettes—had turned into a fiasco. He had borrowed ten thousand dollars from Nathan to purchase the contraband. After the police intercepted the truck in North Carolina, the local driver, who luckily didn't know about my father's involvement, was arrested. My father was stuck with the debt and a crippling 40 percent a month interest rate. My parents couldn't pay Nathan back. It was only after my mother called Nathan, who'd been a childhood friend, that he offered to let my father work off a third of the debt by collecting small sums of money that Nathan's henchmen, the Spratz brothers, were too busy to get to.

"Money," my mother said, "always money, beating me down."

"It's okay, Mom. We'll figure something out."

She looked at me as if she wanted to believe. "How?" she asked. "How are we going to get the money?"

I didn't know. I sensed her fear. In the past she had always been able to charm creditors—summer camps, landlords, department stores—into waiting a little longer for their money. But this was the Mob.


My mother got up from the table and went to her bedroom. She retreated to bed like she usually did when she was upset. It was there, lying in her half-slip in the humid heat that I watched her talking to herself as I stood in the doorway. When she got like that it always hurt me. Her sadness weighed me down. The air got thick. I had trouble breathing.

I knew her stories well. How many times had she told me how stupid my father was? How she had to rescue him time and time again after he had lost their savings. How she had left him five times, but always came back, for the children. She banged both of her hands on the bed. I flinched.

I wanted to get her away from her thoughts, but she looked so angry that I was afraid to make my move. Sometimes it was safer to stay out of her way. When she looked over and glared at me, I quickly walked away.

My connection to my mom was so close that it often scared me. Not only could she read my mind and me hers, but I felt her hurt, her anger, as if it was my own, as if a piece of the umbilical cord had not been severed. When my father was angry I knew to get out of the house, but my mother's anger was different—it made me cry. Over the years she had confided many things to me, things people might think inappropriate to confide to a child. An unintended effect of these intimate talks was that I often took on the role of an adult. Another consequence was that beyond the normal love of a son for his mother, I felt deeply sorry for her. She seemed like a wounded bird. I wanted only to heal her.

During the week since my father gave the money to Morris, I worried every day about Nathan harming my father. I worried so much that my stomach began to hurt. I kept rubbing it and looking out the window for strangers. I was afraid I was going to get colitis like my cousin who had to wear a bag on his abdomen.

My father had told Fat Bertha to warn him if any thugs turned up in the neighborhood. I also pestered her, needing to be reassured that she hadn't seen the Spratz brothers.

I was afraid she might miss them because she was distracted at the moment by the feud she was having with Fat Lil, who was trying to steal her power and become the neighborhood protector. Fat Lil dyed her hair blue and sat at her window most of the day and weighed around three hundred pounds, about the same as Fat Bertha, so she easily qualified for the job. But she never became a fixture. Geographically doomed by her fifth floor apartment, she was too far from the street.

The Spratz brothers were heroes of mine, actually. For a twelve-year-old man-child who had grown up with stories of Jews being gassed by the Nazis, the Spratz brothers were mythical, idols. Powerful Jewish men who didn't take shit from anyone. I had never seen them in person, only in a blurry picture in the *Daily News*. But fighting with pillows, I would often imagine I was one of the Spratz brothers taking on menacing foes.

My mother had told me how the Spratz brothers, protecting a girlfriend, Gina, had beaten up seven Fordham Baldies, the most notorious gang in the Bronx. The police, who hated the Baldies, complimented the Spratz brothers and let them go. The Mafia was grateful to the Spratz brothers for protecting Gina, a favorite niece of one of the crime bosses, and Nathan Glucksman was thrilled to find two nice Jewish boys to use as his muscle.

As the days after visiting Morris the tailor passed, my father seemed to grow more tense, and more intolerant of any mistakes I made while writing down bets. "What's wrong with you, are you an idiot?" "I told you not to take bets from Stanley, didn't

I?" "Stop blinking like a spastic." He mimicked me, grotesquely twitching his eyes. "Get out of here; I can't stand looking at you." It was bad enough that I had to stay in the apartment most of the summer days, waiting for bettors to call, missing out on the street games that I loved, watching my friends playing from my third floor window. But then to be yelled at every night by my father for misspelling a dumb horse's name or for making $8 look like $6 because my penmanship was worse than my spelling, seemed really unfair.

"It's not like I'm getting paid or anything," I said one evening, after he called me a moron.

"What you say you ungrateful little shit?" he yelled, raising his hand to strike me.

"Nothing."

"It better be nothing." He went back to undressing, taking off his sweaty suit. I never understood this crazy ritual. He always rode the subway to work dressed in a suit and tie. It made no sense, because he was a cutter of ladies dresses, not a lawyer or stockbroker or businessman. It made even less sense on days like this in July because the trains weren't air-conditioned and at rush hour they were stuffed with bodies pressed against each other. I knew from sometimes accompanying him to work, that when he arrived at the unairconditioned factory loft, he changed into shorts and a sleeveless undershirt—his work uniform. For the next ten hours he stood on his feet, laying out long rolls of cotton and rayon fabrics, reading patterns, and cutting—and sweating. Then he wiped himself down with a towel and put on his suit for the clammy ride home. Each time I saw this strange ritual I questioned him, only to get the same answer. "Mind your own business."

My mother said that dressing in a suit to commute to and from work gave him the feeling of success. Twice a day for an hour he was that person he always thought he'd be and still hoped he'd become. My mother didn't say it in a complimentary way.

"Harry, Harry!" Fat Bertha shouted.

I ran with my father to the window. Wearing only a faded white slip, Fat Bertha leaned out her window, eating what looked like ravioli in red sauce. She held up two fingers, pointed down at a white Cadillac, and then at Joe's candy store. My father waved thanks and told me to wait by the window, to the side so they couldn't see me, and let him know when the men headed for our apartment.

I looked down at bugs dancing in the spotlights above the candy store. Through the greasy plate glass, I could see neighborhood men crowded into green booths, drinking egg creams and milkshakes. Then I spotted the strangers. Their broad backs broke through the plumes of cigar smoke. They stood over the counter where I ate my hamburgers and drank malteds to gain weight. Their hands reached into the ice cold water of the cooler and pulled out a couple of Mission orange sodas.

I scanned the street, making sure no other strangers lurked about. Three six-story buildings formed my block and over a hundred families lived here. Next to Joe's was Henry's barber shop and across the street was Loy Wong's Chinese laundry. Loy was nice but the smell from the laundry was putrid, some combination of Chinese spices and cleaning chemicals. In the afternoons, women dominated the streets, their voices punctuating the humid air; but now in the twilight the men began to take over, inside Joe's, on the stoops, on the corner. Gamblers talked about horses and baseball and boxing. Their loud street conversations drifted up to my window. Horses and sports were pretty much all they ever talked about except every four years when they shouted at each other which candidate to vote for president. Adlai Stevenson had come to Fordham Road in the spring to give a speech. Jack Kennedy, who my mother liked ("so handsome") ended up winning the Democratic primary. Only a few neighbors wanted Nixon.

When the two strangers emerged from Joe's, Fat Bertha signaled me with a quick roll of her hand to move further away from the window. She knocked her plate and a couple of flat ruffled-edge ravioli dropped onto the sidewalk. The men didn't seem to notice. They pushed each other, as they stepped off the curb and crossed the street, finishing their sodas with loud belches. They were huge men in width as well as height. It wasn't till I raced to another window and watched them climb the stoop of my building and open the front door, that I could be sure that they were twins. I was thrilled and scared at the same time. The Spratz brothers.

I ran to my parents' bedroom. My father slammed the door, locking out my grandmother who was walking in the hallway. "You've got to run the bookie business while I'm away for a few days," he said, holding me by both arms. Don't let Rosie take any bets."

"Dad, when I'm outside I can't stop her."

"Don't let her take bets. I don't want excuses."

"I can read the bets to you on the phone." I dreaded the added responsibility of figuring out who owed us money and who we owed. "I have to study for my Bar Mitzvah."

"Don't argue with me now."

When the doorbell rang, I watched as he climbed through

the window in the living room and went down the fire escape. A neighbor, wearing only a shabby housedress, sat smoking a cigarette on the rusted steel landing on the floor below. She fanned herself with her free hand and said something to him as he passed by.

Part of me wanted to go with him. From the shadows beneath the tracks, my father waved another thank-you to Fat Bertha. She nodded her big round head.

The brothers pounded on the door. My heart beat fast and my stomach cramped when I turned the knob, though my father had assured me they wouldn't hurt me. The huge men had large faces the color and texture of walnuts. They were identical except that the man who stood in the doorway had an X sliced into his cheek; further proof that I was in the presence of the Spratz brothers.

Without saying anything, the brothers brushed by me. A heavy elbow bumped against me. They searched the apartment. I followed them as they opened all the closets, looked under the beds and behind the shower curtain. I wanted to say something but couldn't get the words out. Satisfied that my father wasn't hiding they went back to my parents' closet and threw all the shirts, pants, dresses, suits, and skirts on to the floor. Then they emptied the drawers of my parents' dressers dumping all the underwear and socks and stockings and costume jewelry and pajamas on to the carpet. Their thick hands rifled through the bras and slips. When they didn't find what they were looking for—money, I presumed—they trampled the clothes on their way out of the bedroom.

I followed the brothers as they walked past the kitchen where my grandmother was washing dishes. She was singing

"Autumn Leaves."

"You tell your father he better come up with the money he owes Nathan, soon," the brother with the X carved into his face said as he turned toward me. His breath smelled like pastrami.

"Or he'll be cutting dresses with his feet," his twin without the X said, opening the door into the hallway.

"Ricky, invite your friends in," my grandmother called. She walked out of the kitchen to turn on the television. "Come on in boys. Would you like some cookies?"

"Grandma, they don't want cookies."

She came toward us and placed her thumb and forefinger on her thick glasses. "You want some Jell-O?"

"We've got to run," the brother still inside the apartment said.

"What's the big race? Stay awhile. We can play some poker."

"Grandma, go back to the television. This is Daddy's business."

"Daddy's business, what do I care?" I gently nudged her to turn around. She shuffled away.

"Tell your father Nathan is very angry that he missed his payment," the brother outside said. "The only reason Nathan is giving him a second chance is out of respect for your mother."

"I'll tell him."

"What are you, a wise guy?"

"No."

The brother inside the doorway stepped closer. I backed against the wall. As I looked up all I could see was the X coming my way. I flinched when I saw his huge hand swinging toward me. He grabbed my arm. "Don't be a wise guy with us. We're on a tight schedule."

"I wasn't—"

"We'll have some cookies," the other brother said, as he stepped back into the apartment and put his arm around his twin.

"Grandma! Grandma!" I shouted, pinned against the wall.

"What?"

"Cookies! Grandma, bring the cookies."

"Now you want the cookies?"

She went into the kitchen and then shuffled back with a bowl of chocolate chip cookies and Mallomars. "You want some milk?"

The twin stuck his two hands into the bowl and scooped up all the cookies. He put a Mallomar in his mouth and the rest of them in his pockets.

"Grandma, take a walk," the twin with the X said.

"Who you talking to like that?" Grandma said, cocking her hand on her hip.

"You betta get your grandma outta here, kid," the other twin said, pulling his brother away.

I stepped between the brothers and my grandmother. "Come on Grandma, go back to the television. I'll be there in a minute."

She didn't budge, staring at the twins. I pushed her and she muttered, "shtunk… zhlub" and some other Yiddish insults and then she spit on the wall as she shuffled away.

The twin with the X grabbed me and spun me around. "This was a friendly visit. Next time it won't be. Tell your chickenshit father that. And tell your grandmother not to spit like that again."

I stared at the hand squeezing my arm. Besides being enormous and thick and scarred, the pinkie finger had no nail.

The top of the finger had been sliced off.

The brothers walked down the hall. When they were out of earshot and the elevator door closed, I called out: "My father isn't a chickenshit. He's a war hero and you don't want to cross him." That was true, but it was also true that he wasn't here. He had climbed down the fire escape and left me alone to deal with the Spratz brothers. I believed that my father wouldn't have fled if he had thought the Spratz brothers would harm me. And they hadn't harmed me, just scared me. Scared the shit out of me, almost literally. My stomach felt like hundreds of needles were sticking into it.

Mixed in with the fear was excitement. Now that they were gone and I could breathe again, I treasured the images: their massiveness, their belching, the pastrami smell, the walnut skin. This was the Spratz brothers. In my house. Eating Mallomars.

# 3.

Two days after the Spratz brothers' visit, my grandmother held my hands at the kitchen table. Her cloudy cataract eyes looked so big through her glasses. She sang "All of Me" in a quivering voice—

*Take my lips,*
*I want to lose them,*
*take my arms,*
*I'll never use them*

—as if she was ready to sacrifice every part of her body for me.

When the phone rang, interrupting her song, I jumped up beating her to the receiver.

"Hello, is this Ricky?"

"Yes, who's this?"

"Nathan Glucksman." His voice sounded cold. "You're not taking any bets on Dream Away Lodge, are you?"

"No. My dad said you told him not to."

"Good. Don't. Things are on hold now anyway. It may not happen for a week or two."

"Okay."

"Tell your father he shouldn't interpret this kindness as a pardon. I want my money. Tell him to call me."

"Okay."

"How's my girlfriend, Rosie?"

I glanced over at my grandmother, who was gnawing on a chicken bone. "She's fine."

"And your mom?"

"Okay."

"Send them my love."

I hung up. Nathan's message of love for Pearl and Rosie would never be delivered.

"Who was that?" Grandma asked.

"Wrong number."

She looked at me. I could tell she thought I was lying and was hurt, and was going to keep staring at me, not saying anything, so I would feel guilty and tell her the truth. I had seen that look many times. It was useless to ignore it.

"We have to rescue Daddy," I said, compromising.

"Feh, that bum. Why should I help him?"

The phone rang again. It was Mara. "See you in a minute," I said, banging the receiver back on the wall. I gulped down the rest of my Yankee Doodle. More than ever I wanted to see her; not only because of what went on in her apartment, but to escape from mine. "Grandma, I'll be up in an hour."

"Where you rushing?"

"I'm just going down to play. Don't take any bets."

I felt nauseous as I walked past the foul odors of the incinerator room to Mara's basement apartment. In the laundry room Fat Lil, wearing only a flimsy robe, was bent over taking clothes out of the dryer. She shouted hello and I waved but kept walking not wanting her to ask where I was going.

The smells didn't help, but mostly I blamed the nausea on Nathan. I remembered the first time I met him. It was at a wedding; I was eleven years old. He sat at the dais with the family members. He looked exotic, like someone from the Middle East, as he smoked a long cigar and received guests as if the party was honoring him. With big lips and wild bushy eyebrows and slicked back brown hair he was not a handsome man. When he talked to my mother his face lit up. I could see he still had a crush on her, from their teenage days.

As we were walking away from his table, he grabbed me by the arm. He patted his wallet and whispered into my ear, "Ricky, this is my best friend."

I felt slimy, remembering the moist creepiness of his cigar saliva on my earlobe and the smell of his after-shave. I shook my head to clear it and knocked on Mara's door. She opened it and smiled. A fake Christmas tree stood in the middle of her living room as it did all year. Forty or fifty crucifixes and pictures of Jesus hung on the walls. I didn't know if her family was hyper-religious or just needed these symbols to ward off all the Jewish vibrations in the building.

I liked Mara. She was fourteen but looked older. She had plump breasts, shapely legs and hips, big beautiful gray-blue eyes, and a large beauty mark on her left cheek, which she rubbed often, as if trying to erase it. She and her father were refugees from the Hungarian revolution. They had moved in six months earlier when her father became the new janitor.

Except for school Mara rarely went out. Her mother was dead and her father took care of another building in the afternoons, so she was often alone. We had met in the laundry room a few days after she moved in. Her English was pretty good, having lived in Brooklyn for a couple of years before coming to the Bronx, but she didn't know how to operate the washing machine and I helped her. Sometimes, she and I played cards, rummy and a few Hungarian games she taught me. One afternoon in the spring she had suggested we play strip poker. After playing for a few minutes she unbuttoned her blouse and I could see how large her breasts really were, pushing out of her bra. I kept staring at them, studying them, as if I was going to be tested on their shape and texture. I was winning and probably could've seen everything, her nipples, her bush, but I had to go upstairs and take bets from Irving, who called exactly at five-thirty every afternoon.

The next time I visited, Mara put on some Hungarian music and began to dance, using scarves as veils. She smiled at me through the transparent fabric before lowering her fingers and unbuttoning her blouse. She threw it on the floor. The scarves, some solid, some sheer, red, yellow, orange, fluttered as she waved them in front of my dazzled eyes. I stood up and reached for one of the scarves. Mara laughed and allowed me to pull the red one out of her hands as she spun around, exposing her bare abdomen. I reached again and this time she took an orange scarf and wrapped it around my face. It felt silky. As if we were playing Blind Man's Bluff she knotted the scarf, covering my eyes and danced away, but stayed close enough for me to hear her giggling. As I groped I could sense her ducking behind me. She teased me by touching my shoulder, then my calf, back, knee. No matter how quickly I moved she wasn't there when I grabbed for her.

She started laughing loudly and so did I, wanting to see her flesh again. She hugged me from behind. She untied the blindfold and danced away, allowing me to gaze at her naked body as she swiveled her hips and shimmied her breasts.

I started visiting more often.

I had seen my sister naked, taking a bath before her wedding, when I snuck a peek under the door, and one of my friends showed me a magazine with naked women, but images of Mara dancing with her scarves took over my fantasies. I fell asleep almost every night with my pillow between my legs, my stomach sticky, and "Mara" whispered into the sheet.

When we weren't playing cards or Mara wasn't dancing for me, we talked about all sorts of things. I taught her to lock pinkies and say, "Scouts honor." She told me about how her mother died of cancer. I patted her thigh, feeling her sadness the way I often felt my mother's. It felt thick like syrup sticking to me. I told her about all the screaming in my house. How it made me feel to lie in bed shaking as my mother erupted. How I felt her every hurt as if it was my hurt. That was how she felt, Mara said, when her mother screamed endlessly from the cancer. Another time I told her about my sister, who was pregnant but unhappy in her marriage, and how sad that made my mother. Mara described escaping from Hungary, almost getting caught, Russian soldiers with bayonets drawn, who needed to be bribed. The fear still gave her nightmares. I told her about kissing a girl in Spin the Bottle in the dark, how I had ended up kissing her nose. We both laughed.

Now Mara led me by my hand into the living room. I'd

gotten used to the moldy stink that permeated her apartment. Scented candles, which smelled like musk and made the Jesus pictures glow, usually helped. But this afternoon the smells aggravated my nausea and the guilt about leaving my apartment with the telephone unguarded.

Mara was dressed in purple scarves. Large red plastic hoop earrings dangled from her ears. She wore a red kerchief around her hair. Her fingernails were long and painted deep red to match her lipstick. She looked like a gypsy.

Music played on the record player. Violins and an instrument that sounded like a muffled accordion raced in an up-tempo melody. Mara pointed to the blue upholstered chair and I sat down. She said nothing, just stopped the record and started it again.

Her first dance move undraped a purple scarf from her midriff as she swayed from side to side, exposing her milky white belly. Her arms began to wave above her head, her hips and breasts shifting as pieces of fabric fell off her body. As the music sped up, she whirled and spun like a wobbly top. I wanted her to slow down; she was making me dizzy. I looked away toward Jesus, as if he was the horizon.

Maybe I shouldn't be watching this show. Maybe Mara shouldn't be stripping for me. If my mother found out she would disapprove and I couldn't stand her disapproval. I blocked her out of my mind, and my grandmother, too, since she was an extension of my mother.

My stomach felt worse. I wanted Mara to stop dancing but I couldn't find the words that wouldn't hurt her feelings. When I thought she wasn't looking, I closed my eyes. If I could just hold on a little longer, maybe the waves of nausea would go away and

I could rekindle the excitement I usually felt when she danced.

Mara abruptly turned off the music and asked, "What's wrong?"

"Nothing."

"Don't you think I'm pretty?"

"Of course I do."

She sat down on my lap and put her arm around my neck. I adjusted my body so she wasn't leaning against my stomach, which caused her to jump up. "Don't you like me anymore?"

"I may have to throw up."

She brought over a chair and sat down facing me. "Are you sick?"

I shook my head no. "You can't tell anyone." I put out my pinkie to lock. "Scout's honor."

"Scout's honor."

"My father owes some money to gangsters. I have to rescue him."

She unhooked our pinkies and draped two purple scarves over her shoulders, covering her breasts. She placed her hand on my knee. "I have seven dollars saved. You can have it."

"No. But thanks."

"I can bake cupcakes and we could sell them."

"Maybe," I said to make her feel better. "Maybe we can set up a stand by the subway on the Grand Concourse. We could sell lemonade."

"And strudel. And I could bake cookies."

"You're my best friend." I squeezed her hand.

She stroked my wrist as I told her how scared I was of the Spratz brothers finding my father. How slimy Nathan was.

Just talking like this, feeling her fingers gently gliding,

soothed me. I liked our honor-bound talks. It wasn't like talking to boys; I could tell her things that I never would tell my other friends. I talked with my mom about intimate things too, but that was different, that was mostly her revealing secrets to me.

I liked Mara's hand on my leg. I liked her deep voice, her Hungarian accent. The way she kept her watery gray-blue eyes focused on me the whole time we were talking, like I was the most important thing in her life. Just sitting there in the damp dark room was enough. It was quiet and calming. The nausea faded away. Just knowing she cared, even if she only had seven dollars, made me feel like together we could rescue my father.

"You know I would do anything for you, Ricky." Her eyes were huge, so close to mine, so inviting. "You're so handsome."

"I would do anything for you, too," I said. We stared at each other and Jesus stared at us from all four walls. I would've been happy to just go on like this, talking, staring, being together. We could've played a staring game to see who blinked first. We could've had thumb fights or tickled each other like I had done with Roberta, that pretty girl from camp last summer. I could've made her laugh telling her how Grandma had offered the Spratz brothers cookies. But Mara, in her purple scarves and heavy make-up had other ideas. I didn't see her hand at first, didn't see it until I felt it unzipping my dungarees. I had no idea what I was supposed to do so I just kept gazing into her eyes as if the staring contest had begun.

When I felt her hand crawl through the fly on to my underpants, I jerked, startled. Even after she unzipped my dungarees, I didn't realized that her hand was going to be holding my erection. When her hand wrapped itself around it and slid up and down as if her palm was oiled, so much better than my own hand, I was hypnotized by the pleasure. Everything else that I was thinking and feeling vanished.

I let my arms and legs go limp. She slipped her other hand beneath her scarves, between her legs. She said nothing, both of her hands pumping. I was totally in her grip, powerless, but happy when she started making noises. They grew louder and faster, scaring me.

"Are you okay?" I asked, thinking that maybe she had injured herself.

She started panting. I didn't know what was happening; she could be having an asthma attack. What should I do? Maybe she cut herself in there, with her long red nails. I should be upstairs, taking bets for my father, not down here in a windowless basement apartment with my erection sliding along Mara's palm. I saw my mother's face, twisting her lips in disapproval, her dark eyes angry. But Mara's palm felt so good. The pleasure began building again. I moaned a few times. I didn't want to come yet, didn't want this feeling to end. I wanted to stay in Mara's hand and feel the streaming.

I visualized Abe Lincoln, a trick I had first learned resisting tickles. That bearded homely face, his long walks to school in the snow. It wasn't working.

A television jingle played in my brain. Something about being in good hands. Without thinking, as if whispering loving endearments, I leaned forward close enough to kiss Mara, wrapping my arms around her, and started softly singing,

*Running Bear loved Little White Dove*
*with a love big as the sky...*

She looked shocked. Her moans quieted and her hand seized up.

I stopped singing; I felt totally submissive, a puppy in the hands of its master. She re-primed the pump and closed her eyes, perhaps fantasizing that I was someone else. Older. Hungarian. Adept.

This time she pumped and panted at a furious rate. At times she squeezed so hard she hurt me, but mostly I was overwhelmed with pleasure, moaning for her not to stop, just keep going, "please, please."

When I came in a big burst, shooting my stuff a couple of feet into the air, droplets landing on her arm and legs, I felt happy but also embarrassed, hoping she wasn't mad at me for spraying her. But she was busy pumping away at herself until finally she screamed and wrapped both her arms around me, pressing her body against me, the stuff like glue sticking us together.

I rode the elevator up in a daze and floated into my apartment. As I washed my hands I saw my flushed face in the mirror and burst out laughing. Then I skipped into my parents' bedroom and noticed the paper napkin lying on top of the yellow pad by the bed. I held it up in both hands. I could make out some squiggly light-gray pencil marks, a sprinkling of paprika, and stains that looked and smelled like Wesson oil.

Napkin in hand, I marched into the living room and stood above my grandmother. She sat on the couch watching *The Edge of Night*. I shouted over the blaring television, "Grandma, who called? Joe?"

"No, it was Moe."

"It must be Joe."

"I said it was Moe," she snapped and shuffled into the kitchen.

I followed her. "What did he want?"

"What do you mean what did he want? He wanted to take me to the Loew's Paradise on a date. He wanted to bet."

I stretched out the napkin on the table, still hoping I could salvage the situation. My eyes blinked frantically.

"What does this say, Grandma?"

She leaned over holding her glasses, and peered at the napkin as if reading from the Torah. "I can't see so good in this light."

"Do you remember what he bet?"

"It was at Yonkers. Seven and four in the sixth race, or maybe six and four in the seventh. He put eight dollars on the Daily Double."

"On who?"

"A good horse."

"I told you not to answer the phone, didn't I?" I screamed. She looked hurt for a couple of seconds, her fleshy lower lip sagging with a slight tremor. Then she put her hand on her hip and stepped toward me.

"Where were you?" She bumped into me with her bulldog body and pushed her face in front of mine. "Fooling around with that shiksa in the basement? I know what you're up to. You think I don't know?"

"Don't write on napkins," I scolded. I grabbed it and charged off to my room.

"I'll write anyway I want." She called after me.

I checked my shirt for stains. They were faint. She couldn't possibly have seen them—or us. She could barely see anything five feet in front of her, how could she see what was going on three floors below? But she could pull out chicken breasts with her bare hand from boiling water and put a spell on me when she cradled my forehead or fondled my arms. Who knew what other magic she could perform? I lifted my shirt and sniffed. It smelled like Clorox mixed with ham.

Then I remembered Fat Lil. That fat yenta must've called Grandma. "Shit!" I yelled at the walls.


I lay on my bed. Two hundred toy soldiers, some with bayonets, stood, sat, or lay prone on the bookshelf above the bed. I studied the world map on the wall. I looked at Hungary, then Austria and Russia and Poland where Grandma was from. I searched for a place to hide. Maybe Finland? My father was going to kill me. There was no way out. What was my excuse? That I was downstairs getting jerked off by Mara. My mother wouldn't be able to protect me this time. She would be furious herself. Disappointed in me. I couldn't tell her. I could run away to Philadelphia and visit my pregnant sister. I could borrow that seven dollars from Mara for a train ticket.

I hugged my pillows as I lay in bed, consumed by fear. Fear of my father competed with fear *for* my father. The napkin was minor compared to his other problems, but I knew he wouldn't see it that way. He would see it as another betrayal. Me colluding with Grandma and my mother to ruin his life. My mother dominating our lives with her personality and need to control everything. She had inserted her mother into the household years ago, against his wishes, to cook and clean and prejudice the children against him. He once complained that he had enough aggravation being married to Pearl he didn't need another wife. Now his son, who he trusted with his business, was conspiring with the women against him. Suzy too, though she no longer lived with us, was under Pearl's control. Pearl pulling the strings from her command post in the Bronx, getting all of us to undermine him and try to keep him down.

Visualizing Nathan, brought back my nausea. His cold voice played in my head. "I want my money...Ricky, this is my best friend."

I knew what Nathan had done to his other best friend, Charlie Levine. My mother admitted to having fond memories of the times she had spent growing up with Charlie and Nathan, which was hard to reconcile with the story of Nathan having a dispute with Charlie over selling drugs during the mid-fifties. Charlie wanted to. Nathan didn't. According to my mother, when Nathan found out that Charlie was secretly selling heroin in Harlem, he tricked Charlie into meeting him for a truce at the warehouse that he owned in the Fulton Fish market. With the Spratz brothers restraining Charlie, Nathan took a hacksaw and cut through half of Charlie's right arm at the elbow. Then Nathan wept and personally brought Charlie to the hospital where he paid to have the arm stitched back up. Charlie never regained full use of his arm and soon fled to Las Vegas.

I had heard different stories from my mother of what exactly took place and why, but in all the versions, she said Nathan saw himself as the one who had been wounded and betrayed. "'And I was a real mensch, paying for the surgery,'" she said, quoting him.

Even as a child I knew that real mensches didn't go around proclaiming how wonderful they are. Real mensches looked out for others. They exuded kindness, generosity, caring. They didn't ask for anything in return. They didn't cut off people's arms and they didn't induce nausea.

Whether they got hand-jobs from girls from Hungary I didn't know, but if they did they did it after hours. Not when they were supposed to be home taking bets for their fathers.

# 4.

When my mother got home from her canasta game, I wanted to warn her about the napkin. I went into the living room where she was sitting in her half-slip pulled above her breasts, beside Grandma on the couch. They were watching Jack Parr, the volume turned up. But I was afraid if I said anything, she would want to know where I had been. Why wasn't I home? What was I doing in the basement with Mara?

The windows were open but there was no breeze on this hot humid night. I went to the window for some air. Fat Bertha, across the street, was wiping her forehead and Joe was locking up the candy store. Smoke from his cigar rose toward the spotlight as three men stood smoking outside of Joe's, the red tips of their cigarettes glowing and dimming.

I turned from the window, still thinking about warning my mother. My father would be home soon. He had telephoned several times. After I had told him about Nathan's call, he phoned Nathan and then called back to say everything was fine.

"But Nathan…" I protested.

"It's okay. I told him that I'm working on a deal and would have most of the money in a couple of weeks."

"Is that true?"

"Don't be such a stupid kid. It buys me time. I'll figure out the money."

"Where are you going to get it?"

"What are you, Pearl? Mind your own business. I know what I'm doing. I'm getting another shipment of cigarettes. On credit. People trust Harry Davis."


Around midnight I heard my father come home. I listened to him undressing, the toilet flushing, the water running, and then his rifling through the wager slips.

"Ricky!" I jumped out of bed and ran into my parents' bedroom. My father sat on the edge of the bed in his white boxer shorts and sleeveless undershirt, coarse black hair encircling the thin cotton shoulder straps. The napkin vibrated in his hand. "What's this?"

"I think he bet the Daily Double."

"Who's Moe? What did he bet?"

The veins on my father's forehead pulsed as he shot up from the bed, clenching the napkin.

"I don't know. Ask Grandma."

He came at me with his hand raised and I backed away. "You dumb shit," he screamed.

"I'm sorry."

"Pearl!"

"Pearl!" he bellowed again, squeezing the napkin. She rushed in, still wearing her black slip.

"Shut up, you moron. My mother's sleeping."

He waved the napkin in her face. "Look at this."

She swiped at the napkin, knocking against his fist. "Your stupid business, who cares? Don't you care about anything except your goddamn cutter self?"

"Why are you screaming?" I cried. More than my father's hands or insults, my mother's screaming shredded me. I didn't want her unhappy, didn't want to be the cause of her unhappiness. When screams exploded out of her like a geyser, I felt like the world was coming apart.

"I'm screaming because your father is an idiot."

Grandma burst into the bedroom. "What's going on here? What are you all crazy? It's so late. People are sleeping."

My father shook his fist at her and stepped forward. "I told you never to answer the phone."

"Leave her alone," I said. "It was my fault."

My mother moved between him and Rosie. The large mirror that hung above the dressers, reflected not only the four of us but also Fat Bertha at her window looking in. The Bronx night was humid and wet, and it pushed against us. Stifling heat, street chatter, trains.

"I can answer the phone," Grandma shouted. She stepped closer to my father, pushing her daughter out of the way. "Who are you? You're not here. You're out hiding. I'm a person. I can answer the phone."

"No you can't. This is my house and my phone. I don't want you to answer it."

"You stupid bulvan. Your phone? Phew on your phone." Grandma spit at him.

"And phew on your napkin." My mother spit and laughing, snatched and shredded the napkin. I had seen her do this many times before—transform the mood and tame the beast. She would make jokes, pull faces, play with his fingers, fondle his neck, do a little tap dance or sing a favorite song, whatever it took to get him under control.

But this night was different.

He looked at the torn napkin for a second. Then he clasped my mother's wrists and flung her backward against the dresser, the corner catching her spine.

"Ughhh," she moaned, rubbing her back. "That's all you know, *cutter*. Your hands. How to hurt people. How to bully."

"Shut up! Shut up!"

"Show your son what a big man you are, *cutter*. Go on, hit me again." She shoved her face in front of his crazed eyes. He grabbed her and shook. She looked like a rag doll in his hands.

I shouted, "Stop it, stop screaming, stop fighting."

Grandma wrapped her arms around my mother's arm and they both tugged. Grandma looked to me for help. I tried to muster the courage to help her but my father was so scary, so powerful. An artery in his thick neck throbbed. I just couldn't move.

"I'm warning you, Pearl, shut up!" His fist hovered an inch from her face, cocked and ready to go.

"Shut up, yourself! I'm not afraid of you. You're an idiot who can't even make money being a bookie. Look what you taught your son. How to be a *loser*."

His fist crashed against her jaw and knocked her to the

floor. I ran to her, collapsing against her body. Grandma joined us. My father didn't speak. After a moment he stumbled to the closet, grabbed some pants and a shirt, and fled.

My mother threw Grandma and me out of the bedroom. She sobbed loudly and I cried with her as I leaned against her door. I should've stopped my father. Should've tried.

He had never hit her before as far as I knew. They fought almost every day, vicious screaming fights sometimes, and sometimes he threatened her with his hands. I had seen him grab her, seen him push her against a wall, but never strike her. Did this mean she was going to finally leave him for good after all these years? Or would she return again, as she had before, "for the children"?

Grandma came shuffling from the kitchen, a dishrag full of ice in her hands, and opened the door. I followed her in.

"I don't want that," my mother said. Propped up on pillows, she lay on her bed in her half-slip, a book opened beside her. A lamp on the night table lit up her swelling jaw. "Leave me alone."

"You have to have it." Grandma slapped away my mother's hands. She wrapped the ice around her face. "It keeps down the swelling."

My mother glanced at me as I slipped onto my father's side of the bed. "Why do you control my life?" she asked Grandma. "I leave Ricky alone more than you leave me alone."

"Ricky knows how to take care of himself. You know how to take care of yourself? Go look in the mirror. A man like this. Sure, you always knew. You knew more than your mother. Out late every night, movies, theater, canasta, work. What time you go to bed last night? You think I don't see? Three o'clock."

"Why should I have to sneak into my own house?"

"Because you're a bad girl."

"I'm forty-four, Mom." My mother winced, blood slipping out of her mouth. "Aren't I allowed to go out with friends and go to bed when I want?"

"No. Not when I see you killing yourself. It hurts me."

"You hurt me."

"Me, what did I do?" Grandma rearranged the ice. "I'm good. I do for everyone. I go to bed early."

"That's the criteria for being good?" My mother smiled at me. "How late you go to bed?" I laughed and she laughed too.

"Ha ah eh eh eh, a bunch of hyenas, look at you. You think you're so smart, twelve years old and still up at one in the morning."

My mother and I started laughing again on exactly the same beat. "You should stay home and learn more," Grandma ranted at my mother. "There's so much life on television, hmmmmfffff. *The Edge of Night, I Love Lucy*, everything about life, better than the movies. And Lucy, all right, she's crazy, but she's smart and her husband's a prince. A musician. And so handsome, not like that zhlub."

"Desi likes to stay out late," I said. My mother laughed again.

"A real bully from the gutter, and you married him. 'Don't butt in, don't butt in.' I knew immediately. I always know people. That's why everyone likes me."

"I thought it was because you go to bed early," my mother said, beating me to the punch line. We laughed again.

"Heh eh eh eh eh heh heh," Grandma mimicked. She curled her lips bitterly. She thrust her face like a dagger in front of my mother's laughing face. "If you're so smart how come men punch you?"

"Get out!" My mother threw the ice to the floor. "Enough, enough, I can't take this! The heat, him, you, Susan, Ricky—enough, get out, get out!" Her mouth started bleeding again.

I started shaking. She had mentioned me as part of her pain. If I hadn't been with Mara, none of this would've happened. If I had warned her about the napkin she could've prepared a strategy for dealing with my father. If I had stood up to him, maybe her jaw wouldn't be swollen.

"Get out!"

Grandma pushed my mother back down on the bed. She wiped blood off her lips and chin with the rag. "Don't you scream at me. You have to treat me nice."

"I treat you nice."

"No, no!" Grandma pulled at her thin gray hair. "No, no!" She hit her breasts with her fists. "No, no!" She collapsed to the floor. She banged her head repeatedly against the bed frame.

I wondered if the head banging, like her ability to pull chicken breasts from boiling water, was part of some ritual, some magical rites from the old country.

"Why can't you treat me nice?" Grandma said through her tears. "I only do good. Why are you so—" and her voice weakened and whined, "mean to me?"

My mother reached down and ran her hand through Grandma's hair, massaging her head and neck. The two women stayed like this for another few minutes. Grandma sobbed.

My mother stroked. I didn't speak or move a muscle.

"I can't seem to do anything right," my mother said with her eyes closed, after Grandma left the room. "Your sister called me today because she wants to divorce Jeffrey. She's not happy in her marriage. Does she think I'm happy in mine?"

"What did you tell her?"

"I told her to grow up. She's seven months pregnant. Make the best of it."

"I wanted to stop Daddy."

She opened her eyes. "You couldn't have stopped him. It's not your fault; I said terrible things to him." She closed her eyes again.

"Grandma says Daddy is a bum."

"He is a bum and a lousy husband, but he's a good father who loves you very much."

"He doesn't love me."

"You're wrong. He only wants the best for you. He's just unlucky. He's under a lot of pressure now with the money he owes Nathan. He doesn't mean what he says. He's a moron who doesn't know how to talk. He wants to tell you that he loves you, but as soon as he opens his mouth it's like a filter that translates his words into teasing."

She was an optometrist switching lenses. For most of my childhood I had seen the world from her perspective. I was changing, seeing things my own way.

She lay there silently for several minutes. When she spoke again she changed the subject. "Marilyn Monroe came up to the office again today," she said, nonchalantly. I could tell she was bursting to let it out. "I've never seen skin like that. So pale, like alabaster. It's almost transparent."

"Is she nice?"

"We hit it off right away. I've only met her in person maybe three times and we're like best friends."

"Is she nice?"

"She calls me every day."

She loved talking about the stars. It had always been her dream to become one. Though she enjoyed her job, and the proximity to the famous, I knew that it sometimes made her sad that she was only a bit player. She had told me that her job was a refuge from her marriage. The one area of her life where she didn't feel beaten down. She was Cinderella during business hours, dancing with the princes and princesses, hanging out with Marilyn and Richard Burton and Elizabeth Taylor and Rock Hudson and Lauren Bacall and Mary Martin and Sir John Gielgud. Though her boss was openly gay, he still brought her to parties with Otto Preminger and Orson Welles. He knew that sometimes it was just better to be seen with a woman on his arm. She even dined with a real princess, Grace Kelly. But when the coach turned back into a pumpkin she was back in her small Bronx apartment, lying on her bed with a swollen jaw.

No matter how much she tried to put on a happy face or tell me that she was at fault for calling my father a *cutter* and a loser, her sacrifices weighed her down. I didn't want her to fall into one of her depressions. What if she couldn't take it anymore— the losses and disappointments, her potential unfulfilled—and she decided to leave him? What would happen to our family, and me?

"Maybe Marilyn could loan you money to pay back

Nathan," I said.

"It wouldn't be good for our friendship. My boss wouldn't like it either."

"How are we going to get the money?"

"With all our problems we're still the best family in the Bronx." She nodded her head, as if agreeing with herself.

"I'll get it."

"You're going to get it?"

"Dream Away Lodge."

My mother's face froze. She didn't trust Nathan. Wanting to protect his investment, he had warned us not to take any bets on the chestnut stallion, nor bet on him ourselves. He would kill us if he found out we bet on his fixed horse race. When my father had told her about the fix she immediately warned him not to get any crazy ideas.

"Where you going to get the money to bet?" she said, looking annoyed at me.

"I'll get it."

"Don't be a dreamer like your father."

"I'm not."

She glanced over like she was about to lecture me on the danger of being anything like him but paused, gave me another disgusted look, and then said, "I've decided not to invite Aunt Sylvia to your Bar Mitzvah."

"Daddy won't like that."

"He won't like that. What the fuck do I care?" She picked up her book. I knew this mood. "So he could be a big shot, a big sport, he gave away Nathan's money. Jeopardized our family. And you want me to worry about what he likes?"

I clenched my body tightly. "That's not what I meant."

She didn't respond as the minutes passed. She didn't turn any pages.

The air thickened into a pudding, so thick I felt like I might suffocate. I leaned over her and massaged her temples the way she liked when she had headaches. Two fingers on each temple making gentle circles. I felt her sadness in my hands.

"Why did you marry Daddy?"

She said nothing.

"Mom, why did you…"

"How many times do I have to tell you?" she said sharply, and then smiled, breaking through the sadness. "Because he was a good dancer."

She put down her book and turned on her side to face me. "Here he was, a big sport with his pool hustling winnings, the star of the handball court during the day, and in the evening all the girls in the Catskills wanted to dance with Harry Davis. He was athletic and graceful. He won all the contests. The other girls were smarter than me—they danced with him—they didn't marry him."

She laughed, and in a second the thickness dissolved. I laughed too. The air became so merrily light that it went to my head and I felt high and giddy as if laughing gas was being pumped into my veins.

These were her powers. And she could perform them just lying in her bed, with a swollen jaw, and her black half-slip pulled over her breasts.

# 5.

"I'm an extraordinary person trapped in an ordinary life," my mother used to tell me. Though my father was different from her in so many ways, he seemed to believe this about himself as well. And yes, at weddings and Bar Mitzvahs, they did shine. Dressed for ovations they sauntered into the affairs like the royalty they considered themselves. What could the other guests say but "Stunning, what a handsome couple." Sure, the other families had their stars, a good merengue dancer, a mom who could belt out "When the Saints Go Marching In" like Ethel Merman, but could any woman at these celebrations sing half as nice as my mother, who had been a professional singer in the Catskills?

At my cousin Joel's Bar Mitzvah when she sang

*After you've gone, there's no denying,*
*you'll feel blue, you'll feel sad*
*you'll miss the dearest pal you ever had,*

she brought the guests to tears and stole the Bar Mitzvah right out from under Joel, who was busy stuffing envelopes of cash into his pockets.

What about my father? Was he going to let his wife steal the show with one of her torch songs? No way. He grabbed her away from the microphone and wowed the crowd, dancing a cha cha with her beside the half-eaten chopped liver swan. When the music stopped, they smiled and waved at the other guests as they strolled to our table, the applause growing louder.

That night as my parents climbed into bed, I overheard them reminiscing. My father said, "That really was quite a cha cha." After a long pause, my mother said, "We made the affair."

She was joking but I think she believed it all the same. Which was why my father's latest screwup was so disheartening.

Why did you marry Daddy? I asked her many times. Was it really the dancing? I knew so little about my father and almost everything I did know about him and his family came from my mother.

Years before I was born my father's sister, Hannah, climbed to the roof of the Lewis Morris building, once the tallest building in the Bronx, over thirteen stories high, and jumped. My mother told me that Hannah was the only sane sister. My father had eight other sisters, each loonier than the next.

Aunt Ruthie was a kleptomaniac, which made visiting her apartment on the Grand Concourse pleasant, because her closets were full of wonderful merchandise—hundreds and hundreds of knives, lighters, ashtrays, pens, brushes, and her collection of corkscrews from all over the world. For my parents' fifteenth wedding anniversary, Aunt Ruthie gave them a beautiful Chinese porcelain vase that my father had brought back from the war and she had stolen from our apartment a few years earlier.

Aunt Flo liked to be operated on. This need was so compulsive that she developed real diseases: kidney stones and gallstones and malignant tumors. When she finally died in her late seventies she had had fifty-two surgeries.

Aunt Ethel wasn't clinically insane, but her high opinion of herself and her transparent belief that she was right and you were wrong, made her, at the very least, insufferable. She and my mother didn't speak for seven years after she burst into the maternity ward an hour after I was born, slapped her hands together and shouted, "Pearl, Pearl, that is the ugliest baby I ever saw. He looks like a monkey. Some kind of monster. What happened?"

My mother told me that I didn't look that different than other babies, but with the blood disease (an hereditary anemia) my skin was a little yellow, my eyes jaundiced, and I weighed only five pounds. So maybe my picture wasn't going to be on Gerber baby food jars. My mother had gone through a difficult labor, and it was August and hot, and probably not the best time for Aunt Ethel to be her normal insensitive self and shout her verdict: Monkey! Monster!

"Get the fuck out of here you sick crazy pathetic fuck," my mother screamed from her bed.

"Pearl, why are you talking like this to me? I come all the way from Brooklyn, two hours on subways, and this is how I'm treated by my brother's wife."

"Get the fuck out of here you sick crazy pathetic fuck," my mother screamed over and over. Nurses came running first, then the doctor with a tranquilizer.

Before he injected the sedative, Aunt Ethel demanded an apology. When my mother told me the story she performed it, standing up, perfectly imitating Aunt Ethel, her stooped shoulders, her fleshy lips, hovering over the hospital bed, grabbing the doctor's wrist, not allowing him to inject his patient. "I'm waiting, Pearl."

"I apologize for calling you a sick crazy pathetic fuck; now get the fuck out of here you constipated fucking lunatic."

My mother always said Aunt Roz was the nuttiest of the bunch. Before I was born she had lived with her husband and two teenage sons in our building. When my mother told me the story of their feud, there was no performance, no humor. I was eleven and we were eating chocolate éclairs at our kitchen table.

Aunt Roz's younger son, Mitchell, molested my sister with his fingers when he was babysitting. Suzy was four years old. My mother came home from work and knew something was wrong. Suzy didn't say anything at first. "But I knew as soon as I walked in and saw her face," she said. "A mother knows."

Tears streamed down her cheeks as she held the éclair near her mouth. "I didn't want to psychologically damage Suzy so I was very careful in questioning her. The psychiatrist later told me I handled everything perfectly. She couldn't believe I didn't have a degree in psychology. She was amazed how I had the presence of mind to be so sensitive. I'm amazed myself because I was out of my mind. I wanted to kill him. I pretended to Suzy like it wasn't a big deal and waited till she went to bed. Then I went down to Roz's apartment and tricked Mitchell into coming back up. Your father was still at the track. I had closed my bedroom door. I pointed to it and I told Mitchell in a very calm voice that a detective was waiting behind the door to arrest him, but because he was family if he told me the truth, I would send the detective away. But if he didn't, if he made even one lie, the slightest fib, I would know and he was going to prison.

"Once he confessed, I dragged him by his ear down two flights of stairs. I told Roz she had until Friday to move out. She had the nerve to complain to your father. And that moron, I'll never forgive him for this, told me it wasn't right to kick his sister out of the building. All of them, the whole crazy bunch, ganged up on me, said I was overreacting, 'Mitchell is a good boy, a confused adolescent,' and I'm starting an unnecessary feud. 'Friday,' I told your father, and each one of his lunatic sisters. 'Friday, or I go to the police.' Roz and her demented sons were out of the building Thursday night and I've never seen them since. I think they moved to Queens."

She took a paper napkin off the table and wiped her face and eyes. Her mascara bled on to her cheeks. "I didn't want to leave Suzy with any scars. I made only one mistake." Her voice cracked, her breath rattled, and she started crying again. "I never should've allowed anyone from that family to babysit."

Aunt Sylvia had a tremendous need to be the center of attention. She was a real problem at weddings, often dressing up in a white gown. Though she had been grief stricken when her sister Hannah jumped from the Lewis Morris building, according to my mother, she'd also been enraged with jealousy by the headlines of Hannah's jump in the *Daily News*. When Aunt Sylvia wasn't the center of attention she became physically sick, vomiting and fainting—and on at least one occasion, fainting into her vomit.

Aunt Sylvia's son, Joel, was a weird kid. Even the other weird kids didn't like him. He was a tattletale and took pleasure when things went badly for others. But most annoying was his machine gun laugh which seemed to be rapidly firing bullets of venom at you. Once when I supposed to be watching him, even though he was six months older than me, he ran into the street and got scraped by a car. He wasn't badly hurt and I always suspected that he did it on purpose just to get me in trouble.

I knew it was a mistake to get involved with him, but he had that one saving grace—money, which I desperately needed. Having no friends, he spent a lot of time alone building his coin collection. By the time he turned twelve, he'd made over a thousand dollars trading coins. He loved the movies and I figured if I treated him to *The Abominable Snowman* in 3D, he'd be so grateful that anybody had invited him anywhere that he'd be convinced to go partners and bet his savings on Dream Away Lodge.

I walked along the Grand Concourse to his place. The humidity was finally gone. The Bronx looked and felt crisper. He lived in the Lewis Morris building, one of the only buildings in the Bronx with a doorman.

When I arrived I saw a funhouse mirror version of myself, reflected in the glass entrance. I was tall and skinny, with a big nose and prominent chin. My black Keds looked like flippers. I tilted my head and shifted my gaze higher, and tried to imagine Aunt Hannah teetering on the edge of the roof. What was going through her mind as she hurtled through space? What did it sound like when her head smashed against the sidewalk? Was this the doorman who ran over to see the mess? As he opened the door, I was tempted to ask him if he still had nightmares.

My mother had made it clear to Suzy and me that we were from her side of the family. We had been spared the mental illness so rampant on my father's side.

With broken seats and torn carpets and soot dug into the cracked walls, the theater felt seedy. After my eyes adjusted to the light, I noticed that Joel and I and the Abominable Snowman had the only white faces in the theater. A row of eleven black girls in purple 3D glasses sat in front of us. They kept laughing and talking louder and louder to each other and to the monster on the screen. They seemed to be sitting in order of age, or maybe size; the youngest, about four years old and three feet high, sat on the aisle. Every time the oldest, ten seats away, made a joke the laughter bounced like a ball down a staircase to the youngest, who laughed so sweetly it caused the others to laugh again, the laughter climbing back up the staircase.

The Wyoming ranchers on the screen gathered in a barn to discuss ways of capturing and killing the monster that was devouring their cattle. The old rancher with weathered skin and a haunted look was talking when he turned his head, startled by something outside the barn.

"Would you girls shut up," Cousin Joel shouted. "I'm trying to watch the movie."

I slammed my elbow into his ribs. What a moron! A tense silence followed and I could smell fury coming from their backs.

Very slowly, the oldest girl, the one with the huge arms, slipped off her 3D glasses and swiveled her head around, her thick lips pursed in a contemptuous frown. Why was she staring at me? It was Cousin Joel who opened his big mouth.

"You're dead," she said to me and turned back to the movie.

One by one the black faces turned around, each uttering, "You're dead."

Even the four-year-old pixie in the sweetest of voices looked at me and said, "You dead."

"He didn't mean it," I said. "We apologize."

"No we don't," Cousin Joel said, and then let out a loud fart.

The pixie giggled. A couple of the other girls giggled too.

"That's nasty," one of them said.

"You stink," said another.

"You're dead," the oldest girl said to me again. When she looked back at the movie, the Abominable Snowman was roaming through the barn attacking the ranchers.

"We have to get out of here," I whispered to Cousin Joel.

"Why should we leave?" He seemed unaware that he was about to get beat up. "We're not bothering anybody."

I couldn't believe how clueless he was. Being a kid who was constantly picked on he should have developed some radar.

"They'll kill us."

"They're a bunch of girls."

"They're Negroes," I whispered, tensely. "They'll kill us." My eyes darted to the larger girls who I could tell were no longer fully engrossed by the movie, their ears and peripheral vision tuned into Joel and me. "Pretend you're going to get candy," I whispered. "I'll wait here so they don't catch on. Go out of the theater and turn left. I'll meet you in two minutes."

He hesitated. Maybe he didn't want to miss the part where the Snowman stomps a father to death or maybe he didn't like taking orders from his younger cousin, but I didn't care. I shot him another elbow in the ribs. Muttering, he shuffled off. The oldest black girl quickly turned around again but my total engrossment in the film seemed to satisfy her.

I slithered out of my seat, silently backing out of the theater. Before I reached the glass candy counter, the girls jumped up and were chasing me. I tore off my 3D glasses and ran as fast as my legs could go. Outside, the sun bouncing off the white sidewalk hurt my eyes.

I turned left and searched for Cousin Joel behind the building. Luckily the girls swarmed out of the theater and turned right. The plan worked—but then I heard Joel screaming for help. I spun around in time to see his scared face being punched.

"I said left, I said left," I whispered. It was just like him to go the wrong way. Even if it was an accident, it was what he always did, screw things up and make trouble.

I saw the biggest girl's massive fist smash into his nose. Then his body fell out of view and I could only see the girls' legs lifting and kicking. Joel's cries and screams were so loud that for a moment I felt sorry for him. I wanted to tackle the girls and throw them off my cousin, but when two tall, mean-looking girls in purple 3D glasses charged toward me, I ran away. They chased me for blocks. It was just like my recurring nightmare where someone was after me and my legs grew heavier and heavier, and my body slowed down until I could barely lift my legs. The girls must've sped up because the sound of their feet pounding the pavement grew rapidly louder.

When they tackled me, my head hit the cement. They took turns punching me. I didn't fight back. I cried out, "Leave me alone. I didn't do anything to you."

"Shut the fuck up," the girl with beaded braids said before smashing me in the mouth.

I remained silent for the rest of the beating.

# 6.

Except for a lot of bruises and a cut lip, which required eleven stitches, Cousin Joel seemed okay. He and Aunt Sylvia stopped by my bed in the emergency room. She was wearing a fur coat even though it was eighty-five degrees outside. When the nurse came to take my blood pressure, Aunt Sylvia fainted, drawing the attention of the nurse and two aides. While they tended her, I told cousin Joel about the fix and asked him if he wanted to go partners on Dream Away Lodge. He told me no and that he wouldn't loan me any money either. He also said that I was bad luck for him, first the car accident, now the beating. He didn't want to play with me anymore. So I lay in the hospital bed, a twelve-year-old assistant bookie, with two black eyes, and a rejection from the biggest twerp in the Bronx.

"Hi, Mom," I called when my mother arrived an hour later. She gasped at my discolored face and swollen eyes. I laughed to let her know that I was okay. I was hooked up to an IV through a needle in my hand. A heavy, bald black man around forty lay in the bed next to mine, separated only by a curtain. He had stepped on a three-inch nail at a construction site and it had lodged deep into his foot. Judging by his loud moans he was in a lot of pain.

"Hi, Dad." I waved to my father in the doorway, where he stood like a bodyguard. He said nothing, just looked over. He didn't seem happy.

My mother, looking worried, sat down beside me. Her perfume competed with the smell of disinfectant. I pulled on her thick black hair. "It's okay. I'm okay."

"What did they do to you?" she murmured, more to herself than to me.

Just then, the tall, square-chinned doctor entered the room. Either he didn't see my father, who had retreated to lean against the wall in the hallway, or else he chose to ignore him. "Mrs. Davis, I'm Dr. McGinnis."

He smiled at her and spoke in a deep, reassuring voice. He had a scar under his lower lip, which created a secondary mini-smile. "Our tests are negative. Ricky will tell you all about his adventure. He should be fine."

"What do you mean *should be*?" My mother was a nut about health, and I knew that if it took a year or five years or half a century, she would will her children well.

"Ricky took some severe blows. He might have headaches for a few weeks. If the headaches persist or he has any loss of hearing, give me a call."

"Loss of hearing? What did they do to him?"

"Really, he's fine." Dr. McGinnis smiled his double smile. "There's nothing to worry about. I have to make my rounds but it was nice meeting you."

"Just one second," she said. Beads of sweat dotted her cheekbones. "Did you do an encephalograph? Did you x-ray him?"

"We did all the tests. Mrs. Davis, believe me, we examined him thoroughly, as if he was my own son. We double-checked. He's normal. Go home and forget about it." He placed his hand on her upper arm.

Her face turned all watery and soft. My roommate moaned loudly and Dr. McGinnis nodded at my mother before he went behind the curtain to check on the man. He told him he would get the nurse and some morphine. Then he walked by my bed, squeezed my toe with one hand and with his other hand his long slender fingers touched my mother's arm again, as if he wanted to stay and talk, as if he was attracted to her, but duty called. He nodded to my father, who still leaned against the green hospital wall. An unlit cigarette dangled from his mouth. He looked disgusted. His disapproval could've been directed at me for losing a fight to girls, or at my mother for dominating the room, as she always did, or at the doctor for being a high-paid know-it-all, taking all his hard-earned money. It was probably all of the above.

As we left the hospital through a revolving door, dusk was falling. Workers headed home, looking weary. A broken fire hydrant gushed water onto the street, causing the traffic to stall and horns to honk. A breeze picked up, giving me a chill.

"I thought I taught you how to box."

"There were eleven of them Dad. Joel can't fight at all. Nobody can box eleven against one."

"Girls?"

"Negroes. They're not like girls. They know how to fight. The biggest was a monster. She was bigger than the Abominable Snowman."

"What was she? The Abominable Nigger?"

"Don't use that word," my mother said. "I hate when you talk like an idiot."

"You still a nigger lover? They almost killed your son."

We walked the rest of the way, not talking, to the elevated train station. We climbed the grungy steel stairs and waited on the platform. The three of us like strangers to each other, standing apart, silent, looking around at the other strangers and down at the tracks. The station smelled like piss or beer or something else, something acidic and foul.

My mother finally broke the silence. "We're moving out of the Bronx. Right away."

"On your secretary salary? Give me another year and I'll get us out of here."

"Grandma's apartment was robbed last month. Now this. The Bronx isn't for white people anymore."

"It's for your friends...the niggers."

"Teach your son to be a moron like you."

The train rumbled into the station. Its doors opened and closed with screeching and swooshing. The car was half full with dejected faces and an odor of stale sweat. Newspapers were strewn on the floor and spread across abandoned seats. My mother sat down away from my father and me. My head ached and I kept touching my nose, which felt broken, as the train rocked and clanged as we went around a bend.

For my parents, particularly my mother, the Bronx represented everything that was wrong with their lives, their marriage. It was a place of failed dreams, of losers who never could gain a foothold in the winner's circle, of crime and violence and gang fights and reminders at every intersection that they were still part of the lower class. For me it was a paradise. I had friends on almost every floor of my building. And Mara in the basement. There were games day and night in the street. There were young people and old people on my block and always there was Fat Bertha looking out for all of us. We were a neighborhood, a family. And on the corner was Joe's, a candy store, a place to go for a burger or soda or malted.

Looking at my mother, my father said, "Another year, I'll have plenty of money."

"Don't tell me your dreams. I'm sick of them. We're moving to New Rochelle. I don't want Ricky to grow up to be a Bronx *cutter*."

*Cutter*. It hung in the air, almost as visible as the graffiti over the advertisements. *Cutter*. The word sliced me. My father's shoulders sagged, his face drained of color. No matter how many times she used this word as a weapon, its edge never seemed to dull. He always looked pained that he wasn't the millionaire he thought he'd be, or the owner, or a boss, not even a pattern maker.

"I don't want to move to New Rochelle," I said. "I won't have any friends. It's bad enough I'm having my Bar Mitzvah there. Half my friends can't come."

"Shut up," he said, not even looking up. "What do you

know? You can't even beat up a girl. A little mama's boy." He shook his head and then changed his voice to a whine. "Pearl's little pet. Mommie, Mommie, what should I do, that mean nigger girl is beating me up."

"There were eleven," I shrieked. Other passengers looked over. A Chinese man blinked at me. The lights on the train flicked off for a few seconds as nighttime officially established itself. On Jerome Avenue the streetlights and car headlights and the lights of grocery stores and candy stores and apartment buildings brightened the night. Five, six, eight stories high, lights, the train streaking by, the half moon rising above the tracks, and me looking into windows at families eating dinner, watching TV. Normal families who weren't in debt to gangsters. Fathers who weren't mean to their sons.

"Maybe there were two," he said after a long silence. He was good at teasing.

"There were eleven." But Joel would tell Aunt Sylvia and Uncle Eddie how I ran like a chicken and Sylvia would tell her baby brother, Harry, who would look at me again with contempt.

The train slowed, coming into a station. Men and women stood unsmiling on the poorly lit platform. My father waved his hand at me as if to say, "You'll never amount to anything," and then he tucked his elbows against his sides and curled his fingers into loose fists and jabbed, staring at me the whole time. His lower lip rose above his upper, covering it, almost touching his nose and then folding over, exposing the inner flesh, darker, redder, and purplish in spots. He continued jabbing the air, his elbows never leaving his ribcage. Then he emitted wailing sounds and pretended to cry like a baby.

I'll show him, I pledged to myself as I squeezed my eyes

closed, holding back the tears. I wasn't sure how I would get the money to bet on Dream Away Lodge without Cousin Joel but I was convinced that I would. I could see Dream Away Lodge winning the race. See the money in my hands. I'll show him when I walk into Joe's and treat all the men to egg creams and malteds. They'll rub my head for luck and crowd around me as I tell them again how Dream Away Lodge broke from the pack and crossed the finish line first. Then I'll take the elevator up to our apartment and place the winnings on the night table, next to the bets. And watch my father count the money, enough to pay back his debt to Nathan, pay the bills for my Bar Mitzvah, and move to New Rochelle, and maybe even some left over to take Mom out to a fancy dinner at Sardi's.

"Ricky, how could I have ever doubted you? How can I thank you?"

"Forget about it. What are sons for?"

# 7.

Five days later, my mother with her jaw still swollen, Suzy, with her seventh-month pregnant belly, and me with my black and blue eyes, made quite a trio as we sat on a bench at Poe Park, where Edgar Allen Poe's white cottage still stood, surrounded by apartment buildings and stores on Kingsbridge Road.

A continual stream of people paraded before us. Shoppers went from butcher to baker to fish store to fruit market, carrying brown paper bags. Children laughed and shouted as they climbed the monkey bars behind us. A mother yelled, "Be careful, don't go so fast, don't go so high."

Suzy had come from Philadelphia for a visit. She held her hands under her belly as if supporting it. She looked more like our father than our mother, with fair skin, bleached blond hair curled in a pageboy, big brown eyes, and a sweetness in her lips and voice. She was not the great beauty that Pearl was, but she was cute. When I looked closely, I could see a film of sadness over her face.

They were discussing Suzy's marriage. Her husband's wealthy family was, if possible, loonier than ours. The father controlled every aspect of Jeffrey's life, down to what food he was allowed to eat. His father was a juicer. With his assortment of blenders and mixers and squeezers there was no food that he couldn't pulverize into a juice. Jeffrey's mother, though very pleasant, had long ago lost touch with reality. She wore evening gowns every night to dine at Howard Johnsons. They never ate dinner at home. They never ate at home at all—they drank— juice for breakfast and lunch.

Whatever doubts Suzy had voiced before the wedding were quickly dismissed by Pearl as silly and immature. Money—or in our family, the absence of, the dream of—colored everything. A little spinach-asparagus-oat bran-brewer's yeast-liver oil-prune juice for breakfast could appear quite appetizing when garnished with silver dollars.

"I feel so bad. You and Dad gave me everything. Now you're punched in the face and Jeffrey has money. His father controls our bank accounts. It would mean nothing to them and he won't give me a penny for you. He said his father won't allow it. I said, 'What about my father? He's in trouble with the Mafia' and he told me that's not our problem. Why should I stay with him when he won't help my parents? What kind of man is that? If he really loved me he would."

"Give him time. Eventually he'll stand up to his father. Or his father will die."

"He'll live to a hundred. He takes all these vitamins and rides a bike two hours every day."

"So he'll fall off the bike," I said. "Or be hit by a car."

My mother squeezed my thigh, letting me know that she didn't want my jokes now, didn't want me interfering in this conversation. It was too important. Only a master manipulator like her could handle it. Spontaneous with her humor, she was totally calculating in most of her other speech. She rarely spoke without an agenda.

"You're nineteen. Your whole life is ahead of you. During the war your father was away for two years. I sacrificed. I suffered. Things change over time. Part of being an adult is compromising."

"You told—" I started to say and my mother squeezed my thigh again, harder this time. She probably knew I was going to say, "You told me those were the best years of your married life."

"You sacrifice for your children. That's what being a parent is." Her voice gained strength. "Maybe you didn't know that before you got pregnant. I'm sorry, I thought you knew that I left your father five times but always came back. Because of you and Ricky. I gave up my dreams. Everything. For you."

"I don't want to do that. I don't want to give up my dreams and end up sitting on a bench in the Bronx with a swollen jaw."

As soon as the words were spoken, Pearl retreated. Suzy tried to retract them. "I didn't mean that, Mom. I'm sorry."

It was too late. Our mother shut down.

How fast that hurt seemed to paralyze Suzy and me. We didn't move our bodies, barely lifted our arms. Was it an act? Part of our mother's repertoire of control techniques? Who knows?

"Come on, Mom, don't be like that. We're talking. I said the wrong thing."

She looked at Suzy. I was seven years younger than my sister, who was married and pregnant, but for the moment we were both like newborn babies, totally dependent on our mother for sustenance. Soon she would have to let go and speak again, but not yet.

The sounds of the street, which had been only background noise, came to the forefront. Loud mufflers, honking, brakes screeching, shouts of children, old voices on nearby benches, pigeons flapping. A group of small children, all wearing green uniforms, scampered by with two counselors up front and one behind. Four boys bumped into two old women sitting on a bench. The counselors apologized and yelled at the boys to quiet down as the group moved away.

The three of us sat immobilized by my mother's hurt. Then a boy, about six years old with curly red hair, fell from the monkey bars onto the pavement. His loud crying pierced the park chatter and caused us and forty or fifty other people to turn around. His mother and other parents ran toward him. After a few minutes he climbed back on the monkey bars and the communal focus dispersed.

"That's what happens when you don't listen to your mother," I said to Suzy. "You fall off the monkey bars."

Pearl smiled. Suzy silently mouthed "thank you" to me and said, "You're right, Mom. I'll make it work."

"I know you will." She grabbed our hands, her warmth and beauty back in business. "We're the best family in the Bronx. We have our problems but we have fun and we endure."

Looking around at the other families in the park, I could accept her perspective. The competition for Best in Show wasn't that strong. But Suzy was already trapped in a loveless marriage in Philadelphia, and I knew that we weren't the best family in the Bronx, probably not even the best at 198th Street and Jerome Avenue. We were a mess.

"What if you told Jeffrey that Ricky needs an operation for his hemolytic anemia," she said. "He likes Ricky. Maybe he would loan us some money for that."

Suzy shook her head. "He'd want to know if the operation was really necessary. He'd want to talk to the doctor. Get a second opinion. Make sure there wasn't another doctor who would do it cheaper."

"Excuse me," I said. "You told me never to fake illness. God doesn't like that."

"We may have to remove your spleen one day," she said, "so we're not faking it. You don't believe in God anyway."

"What if I'm wrong?"

"It doesn't matter," Suzy said. "He'll never fall for it."

"You don't have access to any of his banking accounts?"

"Nothing. His father is too smart for that. Jeffrey barely has access to anything. He's treated like a little boy."

"Don't worry about it." She patted my sister's belly. "You have more important things to think about. Let's go shoplift some clothes at Alexander's."

"Mom, please. That's so embarrassing. My worst memories of childhood are standing in the department store waiting for the police to arrive. I don't want the baby to be part of it."

"If that's your worst memory, you had a golden childhood. With your maternity dress we could hide a lot of stuff."

"I thought you told me you stopped."

"I did. Almost a year. But with all the anxiety over Nathan and the money, I started up again last week." She looked away from us. She looked like she was watching the people on the street, the women in summer dresses, the young mothers wheeling baby carriages. "Would you rather I start smoking again?"

"When the baby's born promise me you'll stop. I don't want my child to have a grandmother who's a shoplifter."

"Deal, but you come with me now. You're such a great cover."

"If Jeffrey ever found out he'd never let me see you."

"He'll never know. Come." She rose to her feet. Using both arms she helped lift Suzy up. I stayed seated.

"I'll see you later," I said, waving goodbye. "Somebody in this family has to take care of business."

I sat on the bench for another fifteen minutes dreaming of Dream Away Lodge. Nathan called in the morning to let us know that the fix was set for Friday, only three days away. He reminded us not to take any bets or bet ourselves. But all I could think of was getting money. Mara and I were going to sell strudel by the subway tomorrow. That could raise ten or twenty dollars. Maybe I could charge admission for some friends to see Mara perform her gypsy dance. If she was willing I could split the money with her and bet my share on Dream Away Lodge at sixty-to-one.

Lost in my dreams, I didn't notice the Spratz brothers until they sat down, sandwiching me between them. I felt their weight as they pressed against my skinny body.

"I'd hate to see the other guy," Larry said, pointing at my black eyes.

I tilted my head and smiled slightly, implying that he was right and I was too modest to brag about the damage I had done. It didn't feel like a total lie since I didn't speak and there was no guy involved anyway.

"How's it going?" Sam asked.

"Fine. How are you?"

"Not so good," Larry said. "Nathan's angry with us. Says we're being played for suckers. He's going out of his way to warn your father about Dream Away Lodge and your father repays that kindness by ducking us."

"Hiding from us," Sam said.

"Nathan wants his money," Larry said.

"All of it," Sam said. "Tell your father he doesn't want us to have to come down to the garment center and chat with him."

"My dad's working on getting the money." I stared straight ahead at the cars driving by. "I have an appointment with the rabbi. We're making a record at Woolworth's for my Bar Mitzvah Haftorah. I've gotta run."

Sam put his arm out in front of me and blocked my exit. "Who was that girl you knocked up that you were sitting with?"

I said nothing, leaning away from his arm.

"That's alright kid," Larry said. "Sam's only joshing around. We know it's your sister. We followed her and your mother to Alexander's. They've got money to shop but not pay off Nathan. How do you think that makes him feel?"

"They're not buying anything."

"Now, you're a smart kid," Larry said. He placed his hand on my left shoulder and pressed his thumb down with enough force on a pressure point to force me to keel over. "Why don't you run along and convince your father to get us our money."

"And don't mouth off to the rabbi," Sam said. He pressed his thumb down hard on my right shoulder.

Because I was unable to make any progress memorizing my Haftorah, the Hebrew speech I had to give at my Bar Mitzvah, Rabbi Skulnick kindly volunteered to meet me at Woolworth's to make a record. He said that if I listened to it at night before I went to bed, it would help me memorize my speech.

I wasn't a star student at Hebrew School or a devoted Jew or even someone who believed in God, so I thought this was particularly generous of the rabbi. Most of our previous contact had been him asking me if I knew the answer to a question about the Torah and me shaking my head no. My parents weren't religious and attended synagogue only once a year on the high holy day, Yom Kippur. The Ten Commandments, particularly, the eighth commandment, "You shall not steal" wasn't part of our everyday life. We did keep a kosher home, but that was only because of my grandmother and only during the week. On the weekends when she went to her apartment, it was bacon time. I bought the bacon on Saturday and on Sunday morning my mother and I ate it. That was about as close as we came to a Sabbath ritual. Judaism, keeping kosher—even God—were only emblems that my parents wore like tattoos—skin deep, never penetrating to their cores. So why were they spending thousands of dollars they didn't have to throw a lavish Bar Mitzvah for me?

What was important to them, I thought, what did root itself deep within, was the desire that all of their Bar Mitzvah guests would go home saying, "That Harry and Pearl really know how to throw an affair." This need was so much a part of both my parents that the fact they already were in debt to a gangster didn't stop them from planning the "best Bar Mitzvah in the Bronx," with a reception in New Rochelle. And the fact that my father was hiding at Aunt Bella's and the Spratz brothers were making threats hadn't deterred my mother from calling Nathan to borrow three thousand dollars more for the Bar Mitzvah. Nathan, according to her, understood. I didn't. I had smelled the Spratz brothers' pastrami breath, seen their walnut skin, felt the strength of their hands on my body. How could she ask Nathan for more money? Why would he say yes? According to her, the Bar Mitzvah was separate, sacred, and too important to let any other financial issues get in the way.

"Pearl, you drive me crazy," Nathan had said. "That loser husband of yours, I may have to hurt him, but I can't turn you down on this. God would punish me. I'm going to give you a deal because I love you, only ten percent a month, but don't fool around. You have to pay me back."

The first time my mother told me about this conversation, she left out Nathan's parting words to her: "There's more than one way to pay me back."


I met Rabbi Skulnick at the Woolworth's on Fordham Road. It was the same Woolworth's where I shoplifted two pens when I was ten. Shoplifting was a family tradition, but I wasn't cut out for it. Filled with guilt, I dropped the pens down a sewer before I got home.

There were aisles of toys, school supplies, underwear, tools, fabric, stationary, rubber balls, locks, pesticides, beach balls, curlers. Besides the sundries and tempting button candy, this Woolworth's had a one-hundred-foot long breakfast and lunch counter, a photo booth, and a two-dollar recording booth.

The rabbi was several inches shorter than me, a squat man with droopy cheeks, a receding hairline, and heavy eyelids that were always half closed. "I'll treat you to an egg cream," he said when I arrived ten minutes late.

The long black counter was busy with waitresses scurrying and customers occupying all of the red and green stools. The intoxicating smell of bacon frying mixed with the scent of hamburger grease and jelly doughnuts. Tarnished mirrors reflected the blenders and toasters and the grill and the diners at the counter. Customers drank coffee and cherry Cokes and lime-rickeys and sipped vanilla malteds through a straw.

Two elderly women paid their bills and Rabbi Skulnick and I took over their stools. We both drank egg creams and shared a slice of marble pound cake. In between sucking, I blew into my straw making big bubbles in the drink as the waitresses shouted their orders in loud nasal voices.

With his mouth full and crumbs on his chin, Rabbi Skulnick said, "Ricky, what am I going to do with you? I know you don't study hard enough. You're too smart not to learn."

"Rabbi," I protested, "I really have tried to remember but I'm just not good at foreign languages."

"Exactly my point." The rabbi paused to sip his egg cream. "This isn't a foreign language. This is Hebrew. It's in your genes. Don't you want to be a good Jewish man?"

"My grandmother and mother speak a lot of Yiddish around the house. My brain doesn't hold it, so I only know a couple of words."

"Nonsense." Rabbi Skulnick rapped his knuckles on my head, causing me to spill some of my egg cream on the counter. "You're a Jew. Start acting like one. Enough of this punchball and stickball. I want you reading Hebrew every afternoon."

It crossed my mind to tell him that I couldn't because I was too busy taking bets, but it didn't seem wise. "I'll try to do better, Rabbi, but honestly, I'm not the best candidate for Bar Mitzvah. I can't remember Hebrew. I'm not sure I believe in God. I don't know what a man is. I think about it a lot. That part I do good. I try to understand what it means that today I'm a boy and in two months I'll be a man. Is it magic? Does something happen at the Bar Mitzvah that changes me? Are there Hebrew words like abbracadabbra that open doors?"

Rabbi Skulnick looked at me curiously. He squinted his eyes like he was about to say something, like maybe he wanted to get into a philosophical discussion, but then he went back to eating his pound cake.

"Let's make a record," he said, before paying the waitress.

The recording booth looked like the photo booth opposite it, only instead of a curtain it had a real door. Rabbi Skulnick and I shared a plastic seat. First the rabbi recited the Haftorah by himself, then he recited one sentence at a time and I repeated it.

Even with the door closed, the booth wasn't completely soundproof. Some of the noise from the lunch counter got recorded, including a waitress shouting orders. The quality of the record was scratchy, but it certainly was good enough to fall asleep to.

"Should we take our picture also?" I asked. I pointed at the photo booth as we stepped out of the recording booth.

"Why?"

"Just kidding."

The rabbi grabbed my wrist and locked me in his grip. He wasn't smiling.

"This isn't a joke, Ricky. This is your Bar Mitzvah. You have to take it seriously. Becoming a man is the main event of your life so far. Everything you have done and learned to this point will all be culminated on that day. How you handle it, how you accept manhood, will determine your future."

My good feelings about the rabbi dissolved abruptly. I had already been treated roughly by gangsters, I didn't need a rabbi manhandling me. I shook my wrist free and walked in front of the rabbi out of the store.

"Thanks, Rabbi. I really appreciate your help, but I have to run home. I'm expecting an important call for my father."

"What kind of call?"

I trotted away. "A business call."

"What kind of business?"

I increased my speed to a gallop. As I ran with the record in one hand, I flicked my other hand as if I was whipping a horse. I assumed the rabbi was used to decoding symbols and mystical text. Let him figure it out.

# 8.

The next day, Mara and I set up a bridge table by the subway entrance on the Grand Concourse and 196th Street. Mara had baked cupcakes and strudel. I brought lemonade and cookies. We dragged my parents' bridge table for four blocks, nicking the sides against the sidewalk.

I wore my orange and black bumblebee t-shirt and Mara looked particularly appealing in a yellow sundress. We set the table up near the curb about eight feet from the subway entrance, out of the way of people climbing the stairs but close enough to maximize the traffic. We laid rows of pastries out on paper towels. Above us, thick clouds moved slowly across the sky.

Commuters seemed happy to give us business. In two hours, we had made almost eighteen dollars.

"Ten cents apiece," Mara said to the handsome man with an Irish accent. He picked up the last three cupcakes and dropped a quarter and a nickel on the table.

"I think it's starting to rain," she said. She quickly leaned over.

I held my palm up and felt the drops, tiny at first, begin to increase in size and frequency.

"We could take the table down the stairs until it stops raining," Mara said. I looked at her hunched over the food, beads of water on her neck and back, and something tender stirred inside me. I cradled her upper arm and gently lifted her up.

"It's okay."

As the tabletop got wetter, it reeked of stale cigar and cigarette smoke. The remaining chocolate chip cookies and strudel turned into a soggy mess.

Walking home, water dripped off Mara's hair and onto her neck. Our clothes got soaked. But when the rain stopped, a beautiful double rainbow arched across the sky and the cars on the Grand Concourse looked like they were entering and leaving a magic tunnel. Mara paused to ooh and ahh. She put her arm around my back and squeezed me tightly. "It's a sign from God," she said, crossing herself. "Things will turn out for the best."

"They already are." The feel of a wet Mara under a double rainbow washed away any disappointment about the rain. I moved closer and kissed her on the cheek. I would have to ask my mother to invite Mara to my Bar Mitzvah. She deserved an invitation.

Our bodies bumped against each other as we took turns dragging the table along the sidewalk. When we turned down 198th Street, we separated. I didn't want to be seen in the neighborhood hugging or touching. Nor did Mara, whose father would be furious if he found out. Fat Bertha would have a field day and the other kids would tease us mercilessly. Besides, we didn't need to be publicly affectionate, since we enjoyed our secret encounters. It was thrilling for me to have a girl, a nice girl, want to hold me and take care of me. Together we could take on the world: raise the money, solve my father's problems, listen to Hungarian music, eat homemade strudel, and touch each other's private parts.

I put the bridge table in my parents' closet, dried myself, and changed clothes. Grandma had taken the day off to pack for her vacation in the Catskills with her boyfriend, Mr. Fein, so I was alone in the apartment. I spread the dollar bills and change on the kitchen table and dried them with a dishrag. I took out my thirty-two-ounce tomato juice can to count the coins I had saved over the past year. Combined with the eighteen dollars we made selling pastries, I now had over forty dollars. But I had no way to get to Aqueduct and not enough money to make a dent in the $13,000 my father still owed Nathan even if I did get there and bet on Dream Away Lodge. The race was the next day. I felt like a failure. I had really believed that I could save the day. That I could be *The Lone Ranger* or *Zorro* or *Paladin*. It wasn't going to happen. I was just a stupid kid, a dreamer like my father.

A sadness fell over me as I lay in my parents' bed, but after a while I began to see Dream Away Lodge's nostrils flaring again, his chestnut coat glistening as he lunged ahead of the other horses, hooves pounding. I could smell him, feel his sweat. Hear his neighing as he bucked his head. The more I fantasized, the more real it became. At times I tried to think other thoughts, about Mara hunched over the strudel, how her wet yellow dress clung to her body, how she refused to take any of the money. But as the afternoon passed, whether I was taking bets or fighting with pillows or listening to the record I had made with the rabbi, Dream Away Lodge snuck back in. It was a fantasy but it began to take over, as fantasies sometimes do.

My father didn't like anyone touching his clothes so I rarely went to his closet or drawers. But just in case I made it to Aqueduct Raceway, I started looking around for shirts that would make me look older. Rummaging through his closet I found a shoebox filled with eleven hundred dollars. Like in the movies when a guy opens a suitcase full of money, new bills, pretty stacks—only these were old bills, fives, tens, and twenties, tied with rubber bands. Money that my father was probably saving to pay Nathan on the weekend.

I took the shoebox out and spread the money on my parents' bed. The stacks looked like building blocks. I could build a fort with them for the toy soldiers in my bedroom. I could put them back exactly as they were so my father would never know I found the box. Or I could take the money and go to Aqueduct and bet it all on Dream Away Lodge.

The notion that finding the money didn't just happen by accident—that this was meant to be, that I could rescue my family—began to grow stronger in my mind. Even as I placed the box back in the closet and shut the door, I started formulating a plan. How would I get out to Aqueduct in the far reaches of Queens? I couldn't take a series of subway trains with a shoebox full of cash and taking a taxi seemed too crazy. If I got there, how could I place my bet? I was underage. Maybe I could use my mother's make-up and my Halloween fake mustache to look older. My eyes were still swollen and discolored from the beating, which made me appear more mature.

Near the end of the day, I went downstairs for an hour to play stickball on the sidewalk with my friends. The teams were three against three, a pitcher on each team and two fielders, one on the sidewalk, and one in the street, darting around moving cars. Over the train tracks was a home run. Hitting a moving train was a triple. I struck out twice, flied out, and got a single with a line drive onto Jerome Avenue.

Afterward I went back upstairs and just to be sure I hadn't imagined the money, I opened the closet, took out the box, laid out the stacks on the bed, counted them, and put it all away again. Like an addict, for the next couple of hours I kept going back. I knew it was crazy. If I lost the money my father would beat me with his belt and my mother would be furious. She would see me like him, a dreamer, a gambler. A loser. But if I won, I could save my father and make my mother happy. Nathan had said it was a fix. But if I lost, if one of the jockeys refused to go along, if Dream Away Lodge broke his leg right before the finish line, Nathan might kill my father, maybe me. But if I won…

After my mother came home from work, we sat eating Hebrew National salami sandwiches on white bread at the kitchen table. The ceiling globe with one bulb out cast a dim light. The refrigerator hummed loudly. I toyed with the notion of telling her my plan. Maybe she would come with me to the track, which would solve the underage problem. But I remembered the way she had looked when I'd mentioned Dream Away Lodge. The same way she'd looked at my father when he'd talked about his money-making ideas. Like the land deal in Cuba he'd been so excited about in 1958.

My mother cried as she ate. She said that Nathan had called her office that afternoon and was in a horrible mood. She couldn't calm him down. He called her foul names and said that he wanted at least six thousand dollars by next week.

"'That's impossible,' I told him. He screamed terrible

threats and hung up. He's never done that before."

"What are you going to do?"

"I don't know."

"Daddy has eleven hundred dollars in his closet."

"You shouldn't be snooping."

"What if we..."

The phone rang and she picked it up. It was my father. She told him about Nathan's ultimatum. She said she could hock her wedding ring. I watched her nod. Then she said she could borrow a few hundred from friends. Then she nodded again and hung up.

"He said he could steal a couple of rolls of fabric and sell them to another dressmaker. He could borrow some money from guys at work."

They would still be at least three thousand dollars short. But she told me that this is what they had done before, hocked their rings, pooled their resources, borrowed from friends. And when friends needed money, she was always there for them. Always, no excuses. "Remember that, you take care of your friends, and they take care of you."

"What if we—" I tried again, but I could see she wasn't listening, probably already calling friends in her mind. I didn't have the courage to finish the sentence anyway. I knew she would never go for it. It was too risky.

The next morning, after my mother went to work, I took out the shoebox and laid the cash on my bed. Logically, taking the money was a foolish idea, but I kept coming back to three facts: that I found this money, that Nathan called my mother and threatened to harm her, and that Dream Away Lodge was a fix.

The money pulled at me as if it had magic powers. As if it was a magic carpet I could ride to the winner's circle. I put on a nice pair of pants and a button-down blue shirt. Even with the fake mustache and bruised face, I looked sixteen, maybe seventeen, at best. You had to be at least eighteen to wager at Aqueduct. But with $1,140 I could bribe the cashier. My father paid off cops to let him run his bookie business. What's a cashier going to care if he let an underage kid bet, especially if I slipped him some money?

I took a twenty from the top of a stack and set up a pillow above my desk. I walked over to the fantasy cashier and smiled, slipping the bill into a crease in the pillowcase. I practiced this around fifteen times until it felt automatic. Then I punched him in the stomach and the pillow fell to the floor.


I didn't really believe I was going to get to Aqueduct, but I dressed as if I were. I went downstairs just to see if it was meant to be. It was hot. The sun beat on the buildings and sidewalk. I wasn't used to wearing a long-sleeved shirt in the summer. I felt like I was suffocating.

"Ricky, why are you wearing a fake mustache?" Fat Bertha asked. "Are you pretending to be a man?"

I waved hello. I searched the neighborhood for anyone who might be going to the track. Then I walked a few blocks out of the neighborhood, hoping to bump into a gambler I recognized. I passed the drug store and the bakery and Sally's—a tiny store that sold French fries in a paper bag with a toothpick for ten cents. I was about to turn around at the elementary school when out of the corner of my eye I saw Tony Goostaldi, who was in ninth grade, only two grades ahead of me, but of indeterminate age. Some people said he was sixteen, others that he was in his twenties, just a little slow. I immediately dropped behind a green Chevy into what I thought was a well-executed Car Duck. I held my breath and hoped my shadow didn't extend beyond the bumpers.

"Ow," I screamed when he kicked me in my ribs.

"Why were you ducking me?" he asked. A mean scowl was permanently stitched on his face. His thick sweaty neck and back soaked his undershirt as he stood above me. He wore the same sweaty undershirt all summer long and his muscled arms hung like clubs from his broad shoulders. His legs were short and stumpy, creating a creature that looked like it was all torso, a tall dwarf.

"I wasn't ducking you. I twisted my ankle on the curb. I was checking it." I stood up and limped around the sidewalk.

"You think I have B.O.?" I knew that he was very sensitive about his profuse sweating.

"No," I lied. Actually, his odor was extraordinary. It was foul and intense, like old garbage, a mix of vinegar and a decaying skunk, and it radiated at least twenty feet beyond him.

"I'm thirsty. You got any money?"

"No, I'm broke." I hopped around.

"Don't lie to me, ducker. How much you got?"

"Give me a break, Tony. I only got a dime. I wanted an orange soda."

"I'll give you a break." He grabbed my nose between his knuckles and twisted. My mustache fell to the ground. "I'll break your big Jewish nose." He shoved me against the Chevy, his smelly body crushing me.

I slipped the dime out of my pants pocket. "You wouldn't want to split a soda?"

"Beat it, you little kike," he said, taking the dime and knocking me to the ground with the back of his arm. "Don't duck me anymore. I don't like it."

"I wasn't ducking you, Tony." I picked up the mustache and limped away. "Why would I do that? You're my friend."

"Am I invited to your Bar Mitzvah?"

"Of course." I couldn't invite him. He would hit me up for my Bar Mitzvah money. Girls would hide in the bathroom so they wouldn't have to dance with him. Aunt Sylvia would vomit just smelling him.

But Tony could drive. He often stole cars to go cruising for girls. The idea popped into my mind and before I had time to reject it, to remember all the times he had bullied me, I said, "Hey Tony, I have to deliver a package from my father to someone at Aqueduct. I'll pay you twenty dollars to drive me there."

He looked at me like I was crazy. "When?"

"Right now."

"Pick a car." He waved to the cars parked along the street.

"I gotta get the package. I'll meet you back here in fifteen minutes."

I ran home—the limp miraculously disappearing—up the three flights of stairs, heart pounding, stomach nerves kicking, and my brain high on the ether of the dream. I had made it happen. Willed it. China. This was my China. Like my father riding in his jeep through Chinese villages exchanging money at different rates, making a fortune, I was a young man with dreams and schemes and the power to make them come true. I knew about money and odds and horses and opportunities.

I knew about crooked jockeys and fixes. All those hours confined to my apartment, taking bets, learning the business, were going to pay off. This was a sure thing. I was the bookie's son.

But when I walked into my room and saw the cash still spread out on the bed, I was overcome with fright. This was a mistake. It was too much money. Too much risk. Tony was too dangerous. But he was waiting, and Nathan wanted his $6,000. It was just fear, I told myself. I have to be brave. I have to get some money before the Spratz brothers get my father. I scooped the cash into the box.

## 9.

The ticket taker at Aqueduct was a skinny old guy with rotting teeth. He was smoking and listening to a portable radio with a tall antenna and barely looked at Tony and me. The track was huge, much larger than I had imagined, with a massive grandstand. All around us men were smoking cigars and waving their arms and pleading with God to grant them this moment. Men, thousands of them, stood in the hot sun in pockets of three and four, circling numbers on racing forms, tearing tickets, shouting picks to each other in hoarse voices, each appearing to believe he was a great handicapper and the guy next to him was a schmuck. If the chosen horse lost, these men shouted curses filled with cries of bad luck and crooked jockeys. Here and there in the stands was a woman, but mostly there were men.

While many people, including Tony, were lined up at the $2 windows, only one man was ahead of me when I snuck over to the $100 line at the far end of the crowded betting area. The woman behind the cashier's window had bright red lipstick and a sagging chin. I stood there with my shoebox in both hands. I had taped it shut with duct tape so Tony wouldn't be tempted to look in. The high of the dream, the excitement of being at the track, came crashing down as the thought that I might lose came into my mind. After the man placed his bet I tried to step forward but I couldn't—just like I couldn't lift my legs when the black girls were chasing me, like I couldn't stop my father from punching my mother. I couldn't bear to see my mother's face if Dream Away Lodge lost. She would look at me with such hurt and disappointment. She would see me as a failure, a person of *bad judgment*. But after all I had done to get here, it seemed crazy not to place the bet. I started scraping off the tape.

Two men lined up behind me. The cashier stared at me, unsmiling. I clutched the shoebox tightly against my stomach and focused on her red lips. She waved her hand impatiently and snapped at me. I said I was sorry and walked over to the line for the $2 window.

I felt like such a fool, such a lowlife, buying five $2 tickets on Dream-Away Lodge. I felt I had to bet something though I didn't even want him to win anymore. "Hey Ricky, what's a bookie doing playing the horses?" someone shouted as I walked back to the stands.

"Hi, Seymour." I waved to the overweight guy in baggy pants.

He walked over in his orange Hawaiian shirt, unbuttoned almost to the top of his round belly, where his binoculars rested. He had large ears and curly black hairs protruded from his nose. "Where's Harry? I don't see him anymore?"

"Working."

"Your father know you're here?" I shook my head. "Don't worry I won't tell. Whoya got anyway?"

I glanced at Tony, who was standing near the railing and watching the horses parade around the track. The words didn't want to come out. "Dream Away Lodge," I mumbled.

Seymour tore up old losing tickets and scattered them on the ground like confetti. "Christ Ricky, what's the story with that bum? He should be going off at 40 to 1 and now he's down to 7 to 1."

"A lot of potential."

"He stinks."

Four puffy white clouds floated slowly across the blue sky. The track looked dry as the horses walked up to the starting gate. I ran my hands along my thighs, scanning the jockeys, looking for the purple and white colors and the number 8. The air smelled of horses and cigars and men. Tony looked my way and I pretended to give the shoebox to Seymour. I hadn't yet figured out what I would say if Tony asked me later why I still had the box.

The horses bolted from their gates. "They're off," shouted the announcer. Tony leaned forward, his mammoth fists clenched as he shook his body as if riding the mount.

"Could I borrow those binoculars for a minute?" I asked Seymour.

"First tell me how much you bet." I knew by his tone that he had put the pieces together— why a twelve-year-old boy, a bookie's son, was at the track. And why Dream Away Lodge's odds had fallen to 7 to 1.

"Ten dollars."

"Why so little if it's a fix?"

Why indeed? I didn't answer. Why hadn't I placed the bet at the $100 window? Dread filled me and made me feel so small. Seymour smiled as he handed me the binoculars. Was he mocking me for being a coward? I put the shoebox between my thighs and I adjusted the lenses, focusing on Dream Away Lodge, four lengths behind the leader. Dream Away Lodge's head was chestnut with a white streak between his eyes. He looked almost identical to the horse I had imagined over the last few weeks, only graceless and heavy-footed.

Dust rose like smoke as hooves pounded the track. Sunlight lit the dust and made it sparkle. Dream Away Lodge dropped to next to last, squeezed out by faster horses. He hugged the rail as if he knew he was slower than the others. As the leaders passed the half-mile marker, Dream Away Lodge fell even further behind. I had made the right decision. I wasn't someone with *bad judgment*.

"Come on Baraboo," Tony shouted. His horse running neck and neck in the lead.

"Come on Dream Away Lodge," I shouted, relieved that he was losing.

With a quarter of a mile to go, still blocked along the rail, he moved to the outside. Then he switched to a higher gear and started flying past the middle of the pack. The three horses in the lead still seemed out of reach but his sluggishness was gone and Dream Away Lodge looked fast as he gained ground. As if by magic, the lead horses seemed to fall back. Dream Away Lodge was catching up to them. Within seconds there were no tails waving in front of him. The buzz of the crowd grew louder as men shouted and cursed. I joined them, cursing myself. I had come all this way, made it happen, and would go home with nothing to show for it, except maybe seventy dollars minus the twenty I gave Tony. I could've made thousands. I could've saved my family.

"And it's Dream Away Lodge in the lead, Windy Fire second, Baraboo third...," the announcer shouted, riding the words like a jockey.

Seymour shook his head. "Christ Ricky, they could have at least faked it."

"They don't have to."

"I know, but they're pulling back. Look at Filibuster. The goddamn jockey is pulling the reins."

Through the binoculars I saw Dream Away Lodge's massiveness. He was huge, maybe seventeen hands. His shiny coat glistened in the sunlight as he strode down the stretch alone, and probably happy, a winner who could've made my father a winner. As I watched him increase his lead to five lengths, I got more depressed. I wanted him to pull up lame, to fall on the track, not hurt himself or the jockey, but to tumble so I wouldn't have to curse myself for the rest of my life. The pride in my father's face when I gave him the money, my mother's gratitude and love, the men in the candy store slapping me on the back, and the retelling years later—it was all gone.

Dream Away Lodge flew across the finish line. I wanted to scream. To tear up my five winning tickets. "How come you didn't bet more?" Seymour asked. I burst out crying. I didn't bother to wipe my eyes or stifle my sobs. Tony looked at me disgusted. Baraboo finished out of the money.

My heart felt like it was skydiving and the parachute wouldn't open.

I staggered through the crowd, the shoebox tucked in the crook of my arm. Sweating, I pushed through the whining, unshaven men with their hairy chests and gold chains. Their teeth yellow, tobacco stained. Their eyes jaundiced, their skin sunburned, and their cigar-stinking mouths kvetching and shouting.

Other bettors eyed me. The signs of a big loser were all there, I was sure: the pale face, the slouch, the haunted stare. The crying wasn't common, but I didn't care. I wasn't a loser anyway, I had the winning tickets. I slipped them out of my pocket as if to show the men staring at me. They looked away.

This was worse than a typical loss. It had been a fix. My horse won. My plan worked, my fantasy came true—only it didn't, because at the last minute I was afraid to pull the trigger. I yanked my hair the way I'd seen my grandmother pull hers. I wanted the pain, wanted to yank my scalp off my head.

This life, this being Ricky Davis, until now it had been okay; but it was over. *Cutter!*

I could hear the word slash from my mother's lips. *Cutter's son!* She would see me as she saw him—a loser. Much worse, a coward, a sneak, a thief, and a loser.

*Cutter!* I stumbled against the wall of ticket booths where the winners were lining up for their payday. My legs went dead and I slid down the wall, wanting only to lie there. This was how my father must've felt when the fireproof pajamas failed, when so many horses and stocks and gin hands didn't quite pan out. So many dreams shattering before the finish line. I was engulfed by gambler's nausea: that terrible sense of loss, not only of money, but of the dream.

I waited until everyone else claimed their winnings, still holding my tickets. Over at the $100 window the lady with deep red lipstick, sitting behind her metal bars, handed out cash to the big winners. She looked over at me kindly when the last winner departed. She knew I should've been there at her window. She nodded as if to say, "It's okay, honey, you'll be fine." I couldn't respond. I didn't need her pity. I needed her money.

# 10.

I turned the key in the lock and headed straight for my parents' bedroom to put the shoebox back in my father's closet and put the whole rotten day behind me. As long as Seymour didn't squeal, my father would never know.

"Don't clean in here," I heard my father say, causing me to brake and shift into reverse.

"I'll clean where I want," Grandma said.

"I don't want you in my room. Don't come in here."

"Your room? You momzer, you don't even sleep here anymore."

I slowly turned the knob and quietly shut the front door carefully behind me. Shit, what was he doing home so early? I decided to go down to Mara's and wait. Maybe he would leave soon.

"You can't stay," Mara said, after letting me in. "My father will be home in ten minutes."

"Can't I hide in your room?"

"No," she said with fear in her voice. "What happened to

you? You look sick."

"Can I use your bathroom?"

"Quickly."

I had held in my pee for hours. I stared at the shoebox, not sure what to do. I looked at myself in the mirror. Mara was right, my face looked waxy.

"You've got to get out of here," Mara said when I came out, shoving me back down the hall.

I left her apartment and went out into the alley behind the building. I sat down behind the trash cans. I waited till it was dark, and then I waited some more. I was afraid a rat or wild cat might come sniffing around the trash. Most of it was embers and dust from the incinerator, but I smelled some rotten fruit. My father was going to kill me. For stealing the money, or for not betting it, or for both. This wasn't spilling a glass of milk or dropping a fly ball or even getting beaten up by girls. This was another realm of mistake.

Each time I started to get up, I panicked. My father could be a *beast*. I prayed to God. I told God that I would believe in him if he could somehow get me out of this.


"You better have the money." My father shouted from his bedroom as soon as I entered the apartment. "Your mother already called the police."

He moved toward me.

"Where have you been? Where?"

"Aqueduct," I said. "I didn't bet your money. I planned to, but I couldn't."

"What a stupid kid," he said. He yanked the shoebox out

of my hands. He dumped the contents on my bed and he counted the money.

"It's all there," he shouted toward the bathroom. I heard my mother flush the toilet. "Your son is an idiot."

We had a family tradition that when someone really screwed up, like stealing $1,100, that's not the time to attack the someone, not the someone you love. Certain mistakes were so dumb, so beyond the boundary of good judgment that they bypassed the need for punishment and moved directly into empathy. Even my mother, who viciously screamed at my father for gambling away their life, for saying stupid things, for being only a Bronx *cutter*, when he really screwed up and lost his China money on the fireproof pajamas that couldn't miss, when he bought the Studebaker stock—what a deal—weeks before the company went bankrupt, when he gave some of Nathan's money to Morris the tailor to go to Israel, she didn't turn on him. She cried and complained, but she opened her arms and gave him a blank check on the future.

Maybe my father remembered that. I thought I was getting a free pass as he walked out of my room. I had returned the money and he wasn't going to punish me. Maybe there was a God after all.

Unfortunately, I didn't make the cut with my mother. She rushed into my room. For her my mistake was probably so incredibly dumb that it bypassed the bypass and moved back into the world of punishment. She charged at me with her hands already closed, her eyes wild.

"Mom, don't," I shouted. She punched me with both fists before I finished my plea. I fell on the bed and covered my face with a pillow.

"You stupid fuck. How dare you do this to me? I have to live with this moron and take all his shit and now you put me through this. No note. No call. I have no idea where you are. You could've been killed by gangs, drug addicts. How could you do this to me?" She smashed her knuckles into my ribs. She punched my arms and legs. I rolled, causing her to miss a few punches. They slammed into the mattress; they belted the air. "Don't you ever do that to me again!" She grazed my backbone as I twisted out of the way. My father grabbed her from behind. She still tried to swing her fists, but he pinned her arms against her body. "Let me go you dumb fuck," she screamed, and stamped her foot on his. He lifted her off the ground and she flailed, kicking the bed, the wall, the desk, knocking some toy soldiers off the shelf, as he carried her out of the room. She swiveled her head back as she tried to wedge herself in the doorway. "I'm not done with you!"

"What's wrong with you?" I heard her yell to my father. "You're going to let him get away with this? After what he did to us?"

"The money's all there. What are you getting so crazy about?"

"That's all you care about—the fucking money?"

They screamed at each other for another ten minutes. Screams that could be heard throughout the neighborhood.

When they stopped, I thought about my father and why he didn't punish me. According to my mother, he had always been a star when he was growing up. His nine sisters and mother spoiled him. The kids in the neighborhood worshipped him because he was the best at stickball and handball. With his winnings from pool hustling he was generous with his friends. The toughest kid on the block, the best athlete, best dancer—back then it meant something if you could say you were a friend of Harry Davis. My mother had told me this often, not to compliment him, but to put him down, to highlight his failure to reach his potential. During the war his Army buddies looked up to him, and wealthy Jews in Tientsin idolized him, a handsome, strong Jewish soldier, a street-smart guy who could handle the currency exchanges in China. That after all those years of triumph he was now only a cutter of ladies dresses and a small-time bookie living in the Bronx, did a lot of damage to his psyche and their marriage, and at times made him an unbearable beast. But that was why I thought he didn't punish me. Maybe more than anyone, he knew about *bad judgment.*

It wasn't till the morning that my mother came into my room and said, "I'm crazy. Forgive me. We gotta get out of here. I don't trust Nathan."


Over the weekend her plan took shape. She didn't think Nathan would physically harm anyone in the family except Harry. But just to be safe, she decided to take her summer vacation early. Harry would stay hiding at Aunt Bella's and Aunt Bella would take over my bookie duties while my mother and I were away.

When Grandma arrived in the Catskills on Sunday she called to tell my mother that the singer at her hotel had an emergency appendectomy and had to cancel. My mother, who knew the owner of the hotel, from her summers of singing in the Catskills, booked a two-week singing engagement for herself. She would perform two shows a day, six days a week for room and board and $3,600. We would leave on Tuesday.

She called Nathan to let him know that after the singing engagement she would have most of the $6,000. "He didn't hang up," she whispered to me as she cupped the receiver. She started speaking in Yiddish. Her voice softened. Her hands moved more expressively. She sounded like she was singing a Yiddish song in a minor key—a melancholy wail.

I heard Nathan talking back loudly in Yiddish. His parting words, however, were in English. "Pearl, I love you, but this is business."

# 11.

My father stayed away from the house over the weekend and only snuck back late at night on Sunday. I had already fallen asleep and woke to the sounds of him opening and closing drawers as he packed clothes. I came out of my room in my red striped pajamas.

"Hi, Dad."

"Aunt Bella is going…"

"I know. Mom told me."

My father grunted and went back to packing. My mother was out playing Mahjong. I stood near my father, who shuffled in his bare feet, wearing boxers and a sleeveless white undershirt. I watched him, looking for an opening to let him know how much I appreciated his kindness and protection the other night. He folded his socks neatly. He packed his starched and pressed shirts as if they were fragile. I didn't mean to but I got in the way when he walked over to the dresser. "What do you want? Why are you hanging around?"

I couldn't find the words. The avenues had not been paved. With my mother it was so easy to talk about things. But with my father each time I thought of something to say I rejected it before the words found air. We had never talked about feelings. It felt awkward. Probably for him as well.

So we stood near each other. The conversation in my mind wasn't going to happen. He closed the small suitcase, snapping the locks. I stood waiting, still hoping to find the words, as he washed up in the bathroom. The door was open and I watched him scrubbing his hands with soap and patting his face. He shaved and combed his hair. He cut his nails. He was a slow groomer who liked keeping himself clean and neat.

He dried his hands again, put on pressed slacks and a button-down shirt, socks and shoes, and picked up the suitcase. I reached out to carry the suitcase for him, but he glanced at me and kept walking. He opened the front door and I stepped into the foyer. He stared at me for a couple of seconds, then turned his head to the side as if someone had called to him from the living room.

"Tell your mother goodbye." He closed the door behind him.

I shivered. *Something bad was going to happen.* The thought streaked through my mind. I didn't know what. Sometimes I knew my mother's thoughts, knew what she was going to do in the future. But this was the first time I sensed that something was going to happen to my father. Something bad.

# 12.

On Monday morning, my mother and I sat eating breakfast in the kitchen. There was a loud knock at the door. Since it was only 7:30, I assumed it was a neighbor needing to borrow butter or eggs. I stood barefoot in my pajamas and unlocked the door. The Spratz brothers stormed into the apartment.

"Get out of here before I call the police," my mother shouted, as the brothers swept by her. She was standing in front of the kitchen table wearing only her black slip.

"That won't be necessary, Pearl," Nathan Glucksman said, as he sauntered into the apartment and closed the door. "The boys will just be a minute."

My mother waved me over to her and told me to fetch her robe. She stared silently at Nathan who stood in the hallway. He was slim and tall and his hair was slicked back with so much grease it looked wet. His eyebrows were bushy. His cologne stunk up the apartment.

The Spratz brothers' heavy steps vibrated as they slammed doors and knocked into furniture. "He's not here," Sam said as they walked toward Nathan.

"Wait outside. I need to talk to Pearl."

When I came back with my mother's robe, Nathan grabbed it from me. I tried to take it back and he slapped my hand away.

"It's okay, Ricky," my mother said. "Come here."

Nathan held the robe as if waiting for her to slip into it. He pressed his nose into the cloth. "You always smelled good," he said, smiling. When the door closed behind the brothers, he stepped forward. "This is bad business."

He escorted us into the kitchen. My mother reached for the robe, but he pulled it away. We all sat down at the red Formica table. Two bowls of cereal, salt and pepper shakers, and toast crumbs were scattered on the table. He dropped the robe on the floor by his feet.

"We're leaving for the Catskills tomorrow," my mother said. "I told you on the phone I have a singing engagement to earn extra money to pay you back."

His fist banged against the table, sending the salt and pepper shakers tumbling to the floor, chipping the glass. "I said $6,000 this week."

My mother placed her hand on his forearm. She spoke softly in Yiddish. He looked at the table and said a few Yiddish words back to her, his voice still harsh.

When he raised his head he seemed calmer, but he looked over at me. He clearly wanted me gone.

Turning to Pearl he said in English, "How much money do you have in the house?"

"Just over eighteen hundred."

He slipped his hand in his pocket and took out a roll of hundred dollar bills. He counted out forty two and placed them on the table. With his palm he fanned out the bills.

"This is my last act of friendship. When I leave I'm going to send the boys back in and you give them $6,000. They don't know about any of this. As far as they're concerned you're paying off part of your debt as promised. We understand each other? You understand, Ricky?"

"That's very generous of you." My mother seemed to comprehend immediately that he was willing to do this out of loyalty to her. She also knew from past experience that his generosity didn't come without a price. I didn't understand what was happening until she explained it to me later, though I sensed that the crisp bills on the table weren't coated with kindness.

"Why don't you do me a favor now and run down to the candy store and get me a soda?" Nathan said to me. I looked at my mother. She let me know with the subtlest of movements of her eyes and lips that I was not to leave the apartment under any circumstances.

"We have sodas here," she said. "What would you like?"

"Cream soda." His voice sounded like it was filled with saliva. "Why don't you sing me a song, Pearl."

She opened the refrigerator door. "I need to rest my vocal chords. I have two shows in the Catskills tomorrow."

He grabbed her wrist as she placed the glass in front of him. "I'd really like you to sing. That's doesn't seem like a lot to ask."

"Of course not." She poured the soda and sat back down. "What would you like to hear?"

She bent to pick up her robe but he placed his foot on it. "That's a nice outfit for a performance," he said. With the light from the kitchen window, I could see her breasts beneath it.

He took both of her hands, twisting them so her knuckles rested on the table. He pressed his thumbs into the center of her palms. "How about a nice love song like 'Someone to Watch over Me?'"

She closed her eyes for a few seconds as if holding back tears or steeling herself. She smiled at me, then him. She shifted her gaze to the wall clock, then to the window facing the apartment across the courtyard where our neighbors were eating breakfast.

She sang in a low voice. He rotated his thumbs along her palms, drawing widening circles. The residue of years of smoking and crying was embedded in her voice. The smoke and tears wrapped themselves around the lyrics, forming a soft casing. Her singing always captured me. Judging from the smile on Nathan's face and the gentle rocking of his head, he felt her magic too.

He slipped off one of his penny loafers and leaned back. He raised his leg under the table and placed it on her thigh. She tried to move her chair backward. He squeezed her hands tighter and she looked for a second like she was in pain. He inched his way forward on his chair until his chest pressed against the table. His thighs straddled the table leg. He closed his eyes and swayed to the melody.

My mother tried again to move her chair backward but he held her hands firmly so she had no leverage. For a second I saw Nathan's toe press against her belly and then sneak back under the table.

Across the courtyard our neighbors looked over and waved. They wouldn't recognize the man in the chair, gazing so lovingly at Pearl when he opened his eyes. It wasn't unusual to hear her singing. Several neighbors had told me it was a nice break from the harsher Bronx sounds: the shouting fights, the garbage trucks, and the trains, always the trains, roaring through the neighborhood. My mother smiled as she sang but I knew her too well to fall for it. She was angry. Her eyes betrayed her. In the dish drainer I could see two knives, the big one serrated. I'd use them if I had to. I would kill Nathan and call the police before the Spratz brothers broke down the door. I would slice his jugular vein if he hurt my mother.

He let go of her hands and clapped softly. "Beautiful. I wish we had more time together. Maybe next time."

"I really appreciate the loan. Harry and I will work three jobs if we have to to get you the money."

"I'm too soft. That's always been my problem. Especially around you." He spoke to her in Yiddish again.

She shook her head. Touched him on his arm. I can't," she said in English. "We'll get you your money."

He stood up and put his hands on her upper arms as she stared up at him. He looked genuinely sad. The bags under his eyes drooped and his lower lip hung open. He massaged her shoulders. I saw the bulge in his pants. He put his hands on her head and massaged her scalp, pushing down a little.

He moved his thumbs lower, massaging her neck. His thumb rested for a few seconds at the base of her windpipe and he pressed down.

"You're hurting me," she said.

"Why would I do that?" With his other hand he caressed her face. "No more favors," he said, letting go. "Don't make me hurt Harry. You know I love you and don't want anything to happen to your family." He glanced at me and then down at her. "Give the boys the money when I leave."

He leaned over as if to kiss her on the forehead. Then he

darted down further and kissed her on her lips. As she pulled away, his tongue like a contented slug slipped out of her mouth. "I'll see you at the Bar Mitzvah," he said to me, as if challenging me. "Try not to screw up your Haftorah."

# 13.

Blessed with beauty, talent, and personality, my mother had a lot of reasons to believe that she was extraordinary. She had high hopes for herself in her early years. In the story of how she met my father, she was twenty-two in 1940, *gorgeous* and *voluptuous*—her exact words—and when she strolled across the lawn of the Eldorado Hotel in the Catskill Mountains, in her white shorts and red blouse, her hips sashaying, her long hair flowing, a lot of men, from sixteen-year-old busboys to the sixty-year-old social director, couldn't take their eyes off her.

Though she embellished the story over the years, its essence remained the same, and I'm pretty sure, based on the way she looked and spoke, reminiscing, that the story she told was true. She was the dinner club singer for an eight-week contract, six nights a week. She loved this Catskill world, which she saw as a stepping stone to stardom. With her pick of men ready to cater to her every whim, she enjoyed her afternoons hanging out by the pool or playing handball with the guys. She had a crush on one of the weekend guests, Archie Schur. He was a vice president at the Loft Candy Company. They hit it off so well that he booked a room for the following weekend.

All week she daydreamed about him, mentioning him to friends, turning down other suitors, telling them that her Archie was coming up to see her. "A vice president," she let everyone know, not so much to brag, but because it was so exciting to her that she was being courted by such an important young man. She imagined taking strolls through the woods, past the bungalow colonies, to the overlook of the valley, holding hands, kissing. Maybe at night, after her show, they would take a moonlit ride in a canoe on the lake, fireflies encircling them as they talked about their dreams. She even fantasized marrying Archie, moving out of the Bronx, and buying a big house in Westchester, a house befitting a vice president.

So when Harry arrived instead of Archie, explaining that Archie got called out of town on business and sent Harry up to take his place, she didn't hide her disappointment or her anger.

"What are you talking about?" she said loudly, sitting on a chaise lounge by the pool. "I'm not spending any time with you. I don't even know you. And you can tell your friend Archie not to come sniffing around again either."

"Don't be so quick to write me off," my father said. He stood over her in his black swim trunks. She laughed loudly. Maybe other girls were impressed with his athletic build, but his posturing looked silly to her. "I've got nine sisters. Girls like me."

"Good. It's Dance Weekend and the hotel is overbooked with long-legged beauties. Have fun." She leaned back and put on her sunglasses, as if the conversation was over. She couldn't believe the nerve of this guy. And Archie, what a creep to do this to her. She looked around the pool deck at the guests, some of whom had overheard her conversation with this newcomer. They stared at her. There were over sixty wooden chaises encircling the pool, all taken, mostly by young women sunbathing. Her friend, Max, the lifeguard, smiled at her from his perch high in the lifeguard chair. She stuck her tongue out at him. He blew his whistle, confusing the swimmers in the pool.

My father still stood over her. "I hear you're a good dancer." When she didn't respond he added, "I'm going to win the Peabody competition tomorrow tonight."

"Really," she said, laughing. "Who's your partner? Your sister?"

"You."

"I already have a partner. He's the dance instructor at Grossingers."

"Don't you want to win?"

"We're the favorites."

"Not anymore."

She looked at this tall strong man standing over her. He was smug, arrogant, full of himself, and as much as she was still steaming over Archie's classless move, and didn't want to give his pinch hitter the slightest bit of attention, she couldn't help being intrigued by his confidence.

"So you're a professional dancer?"

"Nope. Never had a lesson. Just naturally gifted."

She laughed again. Not because he was trying to be humorous. In fact it was the seriousness and surety of his claims that cracked her up. "Well, I'll be looking forward to competing against such a gifted young man."

"We need to set aside a couple of hours today to practice."

"I'm not your partner."

"Archie said you're also a good handball player… for a girl."

"What else did Archie tell you I'm good at?"

"He said he never met a girl like you. Couldn't find a flaw. That's probably why he doesn't think he's good enough for you."

"And you are?"

"Yeah."

"Harry, you're too much. Really. You make me laugh, I like that, but I wouldn't set foot on a dance floor or anywhere else with you. I like my men a little more modest."

Without asking, he sat down on her chaise, his naked torso leaning against her knees. She slid over a little to make room. She took in the smell of him, a little gamey, but it wasn't unpleasant, mixing with the clear air tinged with pine and chlorine and suntan oil wafting around the pool.

"Look, you're a pretty girl, but I'm not interested in you. I'm here as a favor to my friend. But as long as I'm here I might as well win the Peabody contest. Here's my proposition." He leaned toward her. "Sidney Gluck is the best handball player here. I just watched him play. He's good."

"He's better than good. I've been here over a month and nobody has taken a game off of him."

"Exactly. I'm going to make some money this afternoon by beating him."

She couldn't control her laughing. Against her better judgment she was getting a kick out of this guy. "So that's your brilliant plan? You're going to impress me by beating Sidney."

"See how good we are with each other? We already know each other's thoughts. If I beat him you're my partner."

"And when you lose?"

"What do you think is fair?"

She was sure that he had no chance of winning. She tried to figure how much money she could get from this bragging bozo. She was thinking sixty was too greedy, maybe go for fifty, a whole week's salary for her, and then feeling wild she just blurted out, "A hundred dollars."

"Not very confident, are you," he said. His hairy arm brushed against her thigh. "We're betting on the third game. I win, we go practice right after I'm done playing. Sidney wins, I'll give you two hundred dollars."

The boldness of his gesture excited her. The fact that he doubled down and didn't have to told her that he was either wealthy or generous or prone toward impulse—or out of his fucking mind.

They strolled over to the handball courts. She sat next to him under a maple tree while he scouted Sidney. He wasn't shy about letting her know the weaknesses he perceived. She had to admit that he knew the game. Until he pointed it out she hadn't realized how inconsistent Sidney's left hand was. In order to compensate for this weakness he overplayed his right hand, playing too far over on the left side of the court. Because of his quickness he could get away with this with most players.

She liked listening to Harry talk about the hustle. Instead of speaking with his initial bravado, like he was trying to impress her, he simply analyzed and explained all that he observed. Like a pool hustler, which he also told her he was, he scouted not just his prey but the entire scene. There were four walls, next to each other, with a court on both sides of each wall. Each of the eight courts contained a paved asphalt floor and painted lines. On some courts the men played singles, others doubles, all hitting a small hard black handball against the wall and trying to force the opponents to miss. Sitting in the shade, under the maple and pine trees, were kibitzers and players waiting for a free court. Between the balls hitting the concrete, the players arguing over interference and the kibitzers shouting their advice, it was a noisy scene. "I know this world well. I've played handball all over Manhattan and the Bronx."

"Do you really think you can beat him?"

"I can already hear the cash register ringing."

She looked him over. With his hazel eyes and passionate enthusiasms, he was handsome. His street-smart intelligence also appealed to her.

After watching for almost another hour, my father made his move. He walked over to the court where Sidney had just finished a match. The sun shone brightly and Sidney, who was short, muscular, and partly bald, was joking with the kibitzers. He wore tan shorts, white socks, and black high-top sneakers. His hairless chest looked glossy with the sheen of sweat.

"Hey, you there, you, munchkin boy," my father shouted, loud enough to be heard on several courts. He hadn't prepped my mother on this part of the hustle and she cringed. She liked Sidney. He looked hurt and angry. My father held his ground, dwarfing Sidney.

"How about taking on a real player? Not these pansies."

My mother immediately regretted having sat next to him, as though she endorsed this behavior.

"You couldn't tie my laces," Sidney said. He turned his back.

"Ten dollars says I can whip your ass."

"Make it twenty and I'll bend over."

"You got it."

The beauty of this hustle was that he didn't have to fake it. This part he had explained to my mother. If he played normally but didn't take advantage of Sidney's weak left hand and the tactical flaw he had detected in Sidney's game, then Sidney was a skilled enough player to play him evenly. My father could look like a great player and still lose 11 to 8. Nobody could claim he was sandbagging.

"Double or nothing," my father immediately shouted angrily after the first loss. Sidney stalled for a minute, as if he had to think about it, and then said yes.

The play drew a crowd and my father built up a 7 to 5 lead. My mother noticed that he did this without taking advantage of Sidney's flaw. He winked at her, as if he was just showing off. Then he played a hair sluggish and Sidney won 11 to 9.

Some of the spectators smiled. Others shouted derogatory comments. Almost everyone seemed happy to see my father get his comeuppance.

"Next," Sidney said, dismissing him.

"Two hundred dollars," he shouted to the crowd.

"Save your money, Harry. You're a good player. I mean that. You're an asshole but I enjoyed playing with you."

"Two hundred dollars says you don't even get six points."

My mother made a face. She couldn't believe the stupidity of this bet. The crowd buzzed. "This guy is crazy," one of them said. "How do you know this jerk?" someone else asked her. Even though she knew Harry was hustling, she had to agree. It made no sense. He had blown it. He was too cocky.

Too bad, she thought, because she was impressed with his game. He was as good as he had boasted, quick and powerful, with startling reflexes. The more she watched the more mesmerized she became with his body. She was attracted to him, but only in a shallow physical sense. She would never go out with him. It was Archie who she still longed for. Archie, who she decided she would forgive. After all, there was something sweet about sending his friend up to entertain her and keep her from other suitors until his return.

She had never seen a man move as gracefully as my father on a handball court. It was as if—and she had to chuckle at this—it was as if he was dancing. If he weren't so conceited she would tell him that he reminded her of Fred Astaire, so light on his feet. With that thought, she instantly knew that he was going to win the third game and she would be his partner for the Peabody championship.

But her bet was different from the wager he was offering Sidney. He could win his bet with her by winning the game, but unless he held Sidney to only five points he was going to lose $200. It was a dumb bet, unnecessary.

Sidney immediately accepted. He walked over to the shade under the maple tree and dried himself with a towel. Then he took a clean towel, wrapped it around his head like turban and lay down on the grass.

The men in the crowd started making their own bets with my father. Word spread and by the time the game started there were over fifty hotel guests around the court and my father had wagered over $700. He played the hustle beautifully, my mother thought, still playing mostly an even game throughout the points until at the right moment he forced Sidney a couple of inches more to his left and then he slammed a ball into the right corner. Sidney with his exceptional quickness got to it, but then my father smashed the ball to the left corner. Even when Sidney made incredible gets, diving for a couple of balls, his inconsistent left hand put up weak shots, which my father easily slapped away for winners. Again and again, a slightly different version of this pattern emerged, thrilling the crowd but obviously frustrating Sidney as he became more vocal, arguing over calls and claiming my father was blocking him from getting to the ball.

As Sidney's confidence seemed to wane, my father's grew and he danced around the court like a gazelle, smiling at my mother, a man sure of his prowess, thrilled that he could alchemize fun into gold.

My father served for the match, down low to Sidney's right hand. Sidney smashed the ball like a bullet two inches above the ground to my father's left hand. He scooped it up and hit the ball high off the wall along the left sideline, almost out of bounds, in the back of the court. Sidney raced it down and with his left hand hit a soft shot to my father's right. My father sent the ball streaming down the right sideline to end the game.

"Good game," he said to Sidney after beating him 11 to 5. Sidney grunted and bent over, his hands on his knees. Both men looked exhausted, but my father still strode around the court.

My mother was shaking. She didn't know if it was because the match was so exciting or this man was so wild or because she knew this was all a mating dance for her. Sidney couldn't catch his breath and stayed bent over for more than a minute. He refused a rematch.

In later years, when my mother told this story, she cursed herself for being so vain and shallow. She and my father went on to dance the winning routine in the Peabody championship and when the music stopped she was numb and crying. She couldn't comprehend what had just happened. My father too, seemed overwhelmed. The way he embraced her. The way he looked at her. It was different from before, as if he had a new vision of her. The thought went through her mind that he was handicapping her, sizing her up the way he had sized up Sidney, realizing that this was a woman who could rise with him as he used his street smarts and physical skills to climb the ladder of success.

Neither one articulated their feelings for the other on that night of the Peabody competition, except to say what a great dancer the other was and to share in the accolades and joy of winning. But my mother knew that something magical had happened: Archie Schur was no longer in the picture.

# 14.

A limousine took us to the mountains. That never got old: the thrill of a limousine, the smell of new leather, the polished metal, and the feeling of being rich. The driver treated my mother like royalty. As the private secretary to the top theatrical lawyer in New York, she was in charge of not only which banks the firm's clients deposited their money in, but which travel agencies and limousine services they used. Though she wasn't one of the limousine driver's famous clients, she was in some ways more important.

We stopped for a bite to eat at the Red Apple Rest, with its long red and blue and yellow awning like a front porch and its giant red apple sitting on the roof like a beacon. It felt good to get out of the car, stretch, and breathe in the smell of mountain air and hamburger grease.

As we entered the restaurant, my mother said she wanted to call my father to make sure he was safe. "I don't like it. I don't trust Nathan." After we ordered she used the pay phone near the cashier. I watched her put coins in the phone several times. Then she handed the cashier a couple of dollars for more coins and dialed more numbers. When she returned to the table, she was visibly upset.

"He's not at work yet?" I asked.

"He's always on time. Where is he?"

"Did you try the house again?"

"And Aunt Bella. No answer."

"Maybe he stopped at the union hall or the train got stuck," I said.

She took a bite of her burger. She glanced disdainfully at me. "Don't say stupid things. Don't be like your father. I have to think."

That was the end of our conversation at lunch. Back in the limousine, she continued to brood. The billboards for hotels appeared more frequently. Each one proclaiming the greatness of their enterprise—their golf courses and tennis courts and lakes and horseback riding and famous entertainers and all the food you could eat. This was the country, a cool escape from the oppressive heat of the city.

The hotels where my mother sang, even when she was in her prime, were not the cream of the Catskills. The New Pinehill Hotel was no exception. It wasn't restricted to the elderly, but like neighborhood bars and other resorts, it drew its own crowd. At Pinehill the guests tended to be seventy to ninety years old, low income, and Jewish.

The limousine turned off the highway onto a drive flanked by acres of what might have been sweeping lawns ten years earlier, but was now an expanse of dirt, weeds, and boulders. As we drew closer we could see old people sitting on splintered benches. If ever there was a bunch of buildings that looked like they would fall down if more than three people spoke at the same time, it was the gray sloping dilapidated structures that greeted our arrival. In front of the main building was a big freshly painted blue and white sign: WELCOME TO THE NEW NEW NEW PINEHILL HOTEL.

My mother and I started to laugh simultaneously. Maybe we laughed harder than the joke warranted, but it felt delicious to laugh with her again, to forget about my father and Nathan. She took my hand and clasped it.

Luckily for Pinehill, most of its clientele were on the road to blindness. Those who could see had enough other physical ailments—hearing, urinary, bowel, joint, and an eagerness to tell you about them—that décor wasn't their main concern, though they still complained about the rooms that smelled of mildew and water that never got hot and the frustratingly slow party-line telephone service.

After my mother changed her clothes to get ready for her first performance, we went over to the pool to see Grandma and Mr. Fein. An accordion player was practicing by the shuffleboard court for the two o'clock poolside show where my mother was scheduled to sing. He had long sideburns and a mustache. He looked like he was wearing a toupee. My mother waved to him and signaled that she would be right over.

The pool surround was lined with chaise lounges full of old people. Six old men played poker at a round table under a yellow sun umbrella. Three of them wore visors. Several old women with white rubber caps covering their hair stood talking in the middle of the pool filled with cloudy, greenish water. The women looked like reptiles with their tan pleated skin and eggshell heads.

"Ruthie, this is my daughter, the singer," Grandma shouted to the significantly overweight social director as she passed by. She wore black spiked high heels with rhinestones on them, and a black bikini with black netting over it. Her black hair was sprayed into a beehive that stood almost a foot above her head.

"I know Pearl from years ago." She smiled at my mom.

"And this is my grandson, some handsome boy, huh?"

"Very handsome. You're a good boy to visit your grandmother."

Ruthie rounded up about twenty old men and women to play Simple Simon and led them to a large shaded maple tree.

Mr. Fein came over to us. He was shorter than Grandma and had bony round shoulders. I shook his hand and my mother hugged him. Grandma always accused him of being cheap but every summer he would pay for two separate rooms on their vacation in the Catskills. Usually they would go away for two weeks.

"So who'd you dance vith last night…Mr. Shulman?" Mr. Fein asked Grandma, pursing his lips and flinging his left hand in the air. As if to punctuate his question, a frog jumped out of the pool and hopped over to the accordion player.

"None of your business. You think because you pay for my room you own me? Who do you think you are? I don't need your money."

"Vhy Pearl, vhat's vith your mother? Did I say anything?"

"Oh he's a sneaky piker." Grandma swiveled her fist in front of his small face. "He twists words."

Mr. Fein shrugged and laughed. "I'll hear you sing later at the dinner show." My mother hugged him again.

As he shuffled away Grandma shouted after him, "Go talk about me with the fat yentas. So jealous." Then she turned toward me. "You should see when I walk into the dining room. The men, mmmmhhhhh, they could eat me up. I look so beautiful, not like this. I make up, wear a beautiful dress, every table the men stop eating to stare at me."

While Grandma bragged, and my mother left to rehearse with the accordion player, I watched the Simple Simon game. After about fifteen minutes, twelve old people remained. Ruthie shouted, "Simple Simon says right hand in the air. Simple Simon says left hand in the air. Both hands down. Okay Mrs. Wallenstein, you're out."

The other players stood motionless, their hands in the air as if being held at gunpoint by the local police. Waiting for the next Simple Simon command, their old skin hung like popped balloons.

"Me, why, what did I do?" Mrs. Wallenstein asked innocently, arching her neck.

"You put your hands down."

"So?"

"I didn't say Simple Simon."

"You didn't? I don't hear so good. Give me another chance."

Ruthie pointed her finger at Mrs. Wallenstein, shaking it in slow motion. "Okay, no more chances."

Scary thoughts invaded my mind. What if Nathan did something to my father while we were in the Catskills? What if the Spratz brothers went to the factory where he cuts ladies dresses and grabbed his scissors and cut off his fingers? Maybe we shouldn't have come to the mountains.

If I had bet the eleven hundred dollars we could've paid

off a lot of what he owed. He wouldn't be hiding from Nathan. My mother wouldn't have had to sing to that creep. Or have his tongue shoved down her mouth. We wouldn't be worried that the Spratz brothers might ambush my father as he stepped off the train or walked up to the stoop of Aunt Bella's apartment building.

"Simple Simon says right hand on nose. Left hand on nose. Mr. Fox and Mrs. Wallenstein, you're both out."

"Why?" Mrs. Wallenstein asked, looking shocked.

"Your left hand is on your nose. I didn't say Simple Simon."

"You talk so low, who can hear you?"

"It's not fair," said Mr. Fox, a tall thin man with stiff posture. "If she doesn't go out, I'm not going out."

"Alright, I give up," Ruthie said. "Both hands down. Simple Simon says both hands down. You were all too good for me today. Everyone is a winner. Let's have all the winners step forward for a round of applause."

It was an old trick, but the players were probably lured by the thrill of winning, and they dropped their guard for a second, stepping forward. As they stepped, many of them realized their mistake and grimaced, their worn-out reflexes trying to reverse directions, but it was too late. They were all propelled forward, except for Mrs. Wallenstein, who probably hadn't heard the command.

"Mrs. Wallenstein wins," Ruthie said. "Simple Simon didn't say step forward." I laughed, Ruthie laughed, and some old people on the chaise lounges laughed, but the losers didn't laugh. They seemed quite angry, grumbling and shooting vicious glances at Mrs. Wallenstein who smiled, nodding her gray head as if she was the champion Simple Simon player of the Catskill

Mountains and had just won another challenge match.

My father had to be at work by now. I walked back to my room so I could make a call on the party line shared by other rooms on my floor. I had to wait more than twenty minutes before it was free. I gave the number to the switchboard operator who put the call through.

"Parsons."

"Can I talk to Harry?"

"Not here."

"Do you know where he is?"

"Who's this?"

"His son."

"We don't know. He didn't call in sick."

When I hung up I wanted to call Aunt Bella, but by the time I reached the operator the party line was busy again. My mother's show was about to start so I slammed down the phone and walked briskly back to the pool. My father could handle himself in a fight, but the Spratz brothers were bigger, stronger, and there were two of them. I hated Nathan. His grease and smell and the way he talked to my mother and rubbed his thumbs around her palms. I wished he was dead.

At the pool I sat down next to my grandmother. Ruthie tapped on the microphone set up near the diving board and a terrible screeching sound caused some people to cover their ears and shout complaints. Ruthie spent a couple of minutes adjusting the mike. Then she introduced my mother and the accordion player. The old people on their chaises hushed. The ladies in the pool stood still, their hands paddling the water. The poker players continued their game.

My mother wore a white pants suit with a black ruffled

shirt and a red kerchief wrapped around her collar like a tie. She looked great. The sun was shining, the sky was clear blue, and the maple and ash trees surrounding the pool area formed a natural theater. She sang "On the Street Where You Live" and a medley of Eddie Fisher songs in a minor key that seemed to reflect all the minor Yiddish songs she had ever sung. The audience applauded wildly.

To see her on stage was a revelation. It clearly was where she belonged. She hadn't sung professionally in years. She once told me that when she became a secretary she gave up her dreams and realized that she was a good singer, not a great one. But she could still dazzle an audience, at least an audience of elderly, infirm Jews at a poolside show. She seemed to get younger as the applause rang louder. All of her anxiety seemed to disappear as well. Perhaps it was simply being relaxed, away from work, the heat of the Bronx, and the money problems, or maybe it was the fond memories of her youth—singing and dancing in the Catskills—but I thought it was more than that. For her, the stage was a battery recharger. She glowed, looking fully at home, loving the connection with the audience. I had never seen her so radiantly alive. I wanted her to sing more. If this was what she needed to find happiness then she should do it, tour if necessary. Don't worry about me.

When she sang "Oh My Pa-Pa" the audience totally fell apart, some crying, some cheering. Maybe it was their love for their parents or their love for their children or the memory of Eddie, the Jewish singer who had married Debbie Reynolds and Elizabeth Taylor and sang sometimes at the better Catskill hotels. Or maybe they just felt the heartache in her voice. That's what I usually felt, even when she was singing a happy tune.

Not this time though. I couldn't stop the flood of fears about my father that her song triggered. My heart raced. My stomach, like my heart, had the jumps. Something bad was happening back home.

I tried to calm myself. I decided to call my father again as soon as I get back to my hotel room. He probably wasn't there earlier because he was making a cigarette deal or fencing some stolen fabric. There was no reason to think he was in danger just because he didn't show up for work. Nathan wouldn't have loaned us the $4,200 to give to the Spratz brothers if he was planning on harming Harry the next day. Even my mother had said that. Maybe one of my crazy aunts was sick and needed help? Maybe my father was driving up to the mountains to surprise us?

I shouldn't be losing time listening to this singing. I sneaked off as the audience was demanding an encore. I walked fast, hoping nobody else was on the party line. I just wanted to hear his voice. That voice that often spoke harshly, that didn't say much, certainly not much complimentary or positive. It didn't matter; I just wanted to hear it.

When I got to my room and picked up the receiver I heard an old woman talking.

"How long you going to be?" I asked.

"Who's this?" she asked, annoyed.

"Who's there?" another person said.

"I need to make an important call. I just want to know when you'll be done."

"I don't know, what's it your business? five minutes, ten minutes."

"Hurry." I hung up and waited.

When I told my mother that evening about my fears that my father was in danger, that I had called several times and he never arrived at work, at first she said not to worry and repeated her notion that Nathan wouldn't be looking to harm him yet. Then she admitted that she was frightened too. But we had to put our fears aside. The show must go on. If she hadn't promised Nathan the money she was earning singing, she said she would've called the limousine service and had them take us home.

"Don't worry so much," she said, switching from anxiety back to reassurance, "your father knows how to take care of himself. He's a survivor and whatever danger he's in he'll get out of it okay."

"Even against the Spratz brothers?"

"Yes."

But I could see how upset she was. "You don't have to lie to me."

"What do you want me to say? That I know something is terribly wrong? I don't know that for fact. I just feel it in my bones."

I studied her face. It was all there, the wish to protect me, the desire to be strong, the longing for comfort, the terror. For a woman who loved to play cards she didn't have a good poker face.

"A wife knows."

As I was about to learn, a child knows too.

# 15.

It was after midnight at the New Pinehill Hotel when my mother finally reached my father. His subway train had been in an accident. He'd only been bumped and bruised, but the train was stuck in a tunnel for eleven hours. He was still cranky from the ordeal and didn't feel like talking.

"That explains the bad feeling," my mother said when she hung up. But it didn't. Our premonitions came true with a vengeance two weeks later, after we returned from the Catskills. My father and I were walking down the Grand Concourse on a muggy morning on our way to visit Aunt Flo in the hospital. She had her enlarged spleen removed by the same surgeon who had taken out her gallbladder the year before and one of her kidneys the year before that.

"Get in," Larry Spratz said menacingly as the twins drove up alongside us. The top of their white Cadillac convertible was down.

"Go home," my father said, pushing me away.

"He's coming too," Sam said. He raised his gun above the door.

We sat in the back. My father squeezed my arm. He talked to the brothers in a normal voice, chatting about the sticky day and the Yankees. I didn't say a word during the whole ride that lasted over an hour when we got stuck in traffic near the Brooklyn Bridge. With the convertible top down, the fumes from the stalled buses and trucks assaulted us from all sides. I was already feeling weak but the fumes made me dizzy. I felt like I had the flu.

They parked in front of a long building at the Fulton Fish Market and told us to get out. As we entered the vast warehouse, the overwhelming smell of decomposing fish made the diesel fumes seem like a pleasant memory. The stink seeped into me. I could barely walk. Several wooden barrels were scattered on the floor. Hooks and rusty chains were suspended like decorations from steel beams in the corrugated metal ceiling. Three old round scales that looked like clocks with large metal baskets attached also hung on chains from the beams. As we walked further into the warehouse, I could see discarded mackerel and salmon rotting on the floor and a large decaying tuna hanging from a hook. I gasped when I recognized Morris the tailor hanging from another hook behind the tuna. He opened and closed his eyes three times when he saw us.

My father spun around. Sam took out his gun again and pointed it at him. "Don't be a hero," he said.

My father allowed Larry to tie his wrists together with a rope. Then Sam lowered down one of the hooks, placed my father's hands over it, the rope resting on the curved steel, and hoisted him up until he was hanging on one side of the tuna with Morris on the other. My father's face was now frozen as if he was trying not to reveal any fear or intention, but his eyes told me to stay calm, not to panic.

At least that's what I thought as I stood watching him hang, feeling panic racing through my body. The brothers stuffed their nostrils with cotton balls to block the torturous smells and gave me two balls as well. Then Larry led me to a folding chair in the middle of the warehouse about forty feet from my father and Morris.

"Don't move from the chair," he said.

Not that I could move even if I wanted to, with my arms and legs trembling, the sight of my father hanging from the hook sucking the breath out of my body, and the stink draining me––a stench so awful and powerful that I knew it would stay on my skin for weeks and would linger in my mind for years, like the ether I could still smell from having my tonsils out when I was seven.

The brothers unfolded two chairs midway between the hanging men and me, and using an old crate as a table they started playing gin.

Half a dozen boxes of Excello white shirts were spread out on the floor near me and radios were stacked on top of each other in several piles against a wall at least a hundred feet away. The rest of the warehouse looked empty except for a couple of dirty rags on the floor.

"I'm sorry for getting you into this," my father said to Morris after he had been hanging for about twenty minutes. Morris was white and shivering even though the warehouse was brutally hot.

"I should be apologizing to you. I should've left the country immediately like you told me. I kept going to the track."

My father looked exhausted hanging there as the hours passed by. In the early afternoon I realized that he had wet his pants. About an hour later he vomited on his shirt and asked the Spratz brothers for some water.

"I knock with seven," Sam said.

"Bastard. That's my gin card."

"Water."

"Nathan will be here soon," Sam said. "Then you'll get to drink."

"His piss," Larry joked.

"Or his come," Sam said. The brothers laughed. Larry shuffled.


Time passed slowly as we waited. I didn't know what was going to happen when Nathan arrived, but I feared the worst. I envisioned Morris and my father losing their fingers or hands. Their livelihoods. I thought about bolting, since the Spratz brothers hadn't bothered to tie me up. I could run to the police; but my body was depleted of any energy. I had seen men hanging from nooses in cowboy movies, but watching Morris and my father hanging from hooks, helpless, exhausted, was too painful. I looked over at the Spratz brothers playing gin and I counted seventy-two radios stacked against the wall. I also counted the dead fish on the floor. I stopped counting when I reached a thousand.

Though my father glanced over a couple of times, I had the

feeling he preferred not to look at me either. He was probably embarrassed for me to see him so defeated, or maybe he was just weak from hanging and needed to preserve his strength.

Most of the time I just sat on my chair, alone with my thoughts. When I wasn't trying to figure out how to rescue my father and Morris, my mind drifted to thoughts about my Bar Mitzvah, reciting a great Haftorah, getting a standing ovation from family and friends, walking into Joe's, the men smiling, acknowledging me as one of them—a man. Then moving away from this world.

Finally, in the late afternoon, Nathan Glucksman strolled into the warehouse with a young woman on his arm. He was smoking a cigar and wearing a seersucker suit and white buck shoes as if coming to a party. The young woman yelled when she saw the hanging men and tried to break free, but Nathan clutched her tightly.

The Spratz brothers stopped playing cards and jumped to attention. After Nathan nodded, Sam went over to Morris.

"Wake up," he said, shaking the tailor. "You got company."

Morris opened his eyes. "Rachel," he cried out.

"Uncle."

"Why did you bring her here?" he asked Nathan and started to weep.

"Water," my father said.

Nathan signaled to Sam with a flick of his wrist and a fluttering of his fingers to let the men down and give them some water. He handed the woman some cotton to stuff in her nose. Her hair was auburn and frizzy, her lips thick and lush, and intelligence gleamed in her eyes. She was young and fresh and bold. And shaking with fright.

"I'm sorry, Rachel," Nathan said. "Sorry you have to see this."

She grabbed his hands. "Nathan, I'm pleading with you, let's work this out. We'll get you the rest of the money."

"How? You've had months."

"It's my fault. He spoils me. I'm his only surviving relative. I'll drop out of college and get a job. You can have all the money I earn."

"Good. So we don't have to kill him. But he still has to be punished for what he did."

"Look at him. You've punished him enough."

"Harry, you schmuck!" Nathan turned toward my father who was drinking from a grimy cup of water. "See what you've caused. I could kill you with my bare hands and pull your fucking heart out for making me hurt this lovely girl."

My father slumped in the chair and continued to gulp down the water. He looked down at the floor. He didn't look at Rachel or Nathan or me or Morris who Sam also unhooked and escorted to a chair a few feet from my father.

"I'm sorry. I made a mistake. I was wrong."

Nathan screamed, "Damn fucking right you were wrong. How could you do that to me? Betray me for a stranger?"

"He's a Holocaust survivor. I wanted to help him."

"What the fuck do I care? He owes me money. You're job was to collect it. Not to give him my money. My money, you disloyal fuck. My money!"

"It was a mistake."

Nathan signaled to Larry with his head. Sam took a hacksaw out of his briefcase. We all turned our heads toward it, our eyes drawn to its triangular teeth. Sweat poured down my father's face. Morris began to whimper. As if the blade was magnetized it pulled away whatever steel was left in my body. Larry flicked his finger at the blade and it made a quiet "ping."

Morris fainted. I let out a wail and leaned my head down to my knees. When I raised my head my father was staring at me. He looked so sad, as if he was apologizing. Rachel begged Nathan again not to do this. Sam shuffled the cards and put them back in the box. Then he picked up the crate and carried it next to the two men. Larry placed the hacksaw on the crate.

Sam grabbed Morris and shook him awake. Larry placed Morris's arm next to the saw on the crate. Morris didn't resist. He looked like he was praying.

"We're going to cut two fingers off your left hand," Nathan said. "Only out of respect for Rachel I'm leaving you the rest so you can still make a living as a tailor."

"Don't," Rachel pleaded. She stepped in front of Nathan, her hands touching his hands, arms, chest, cheeks. "Nathan, please. Don't do this to us. We'll get you more money." She stepped closer, pressing her youthful body against him, stroking his neck and shoulders.

"Rachel, I'm sorry. There are rules. People know what he did. I can't allow him to go unpunished."

She gazed at him. Her hands slid down his ribcage. "I understand. But we can work this out. Another punishment." Nathan locked eyes with her.

He strode over to my father. "You see. See what you've done you dumb schmuck." He crouched down and blew smoke in my father's face. "You betrayed me," he shouted. "I did everything for you. I loaned you money. I warned you about the fix on Dream Away Lodge so you wouldn't lose money. I covered for you when you couldn't raise the money. I gave you a job to help you out and this is how you repay me. You fuck with my money. Now I'm going to teach you what happens to people who fuck with Nathan Glucksman's money. What's going to happen to Pearl if I don't get my money."

Nathan sucked on his cigar, blew more smoke into my father 's face and threw the lit stub on the floor. He walked back to Rachel and put his hands on her shoulders. "This all could've been prevented if that man had one tenth of your loyalty. During the war I tried to have an affair with Pearl. But she refused. That's how loyal she was to him. I bought her flowers, presents. All of the married women were having affairs. What did it matter? There was a war. Suckers like him were most likely not coming back home. Pearl couldn't betray him. But he had no problem betraying me for a stranger. You're loyal like Pearl. I respect that. You'll do anything to protect your pathetic Uncle Morris."

Nathan moved his hands around Rachel's shoulder blades. Like a father comforting a child he patted her back a couple of times. Her hair fell over his hands. He slowly moved them downward, resting for a few seconds on the small of her back and then down to her ass, which he grabbed with both hands, pulling her body tightly against him.

"Whatever you want, Nathan," she said.

"No," Morris said.

"Only if you want to. I would never force any woman."

"I understand." She started to unbutton her blouse.

"No, Rachel," Morris moaned.

Nathan lifted her skirt, his hands sliding along the silk of her panties. "Just give me a blow job now and you can pay me back the rest of the money in installments."

Rachel nodded. She took a couple of deep breaths.

"Rachel, please, don't. I can get by with one hand."

"You guys want to talk about it?" Nathan said, angering, unzipping his pants. "I'm trying to do you a favor. If you don't appreciate it, forget it."

"We appreciate it, Nathan, you know that." Rachel fondled him again, her hands slipping beneath his suit jacket to massage his chest. "I'm very grateful. Morris is exhausted. He's not thinking straight."

"He has to watch," Nathan said. "Pull up his fucking head and make him look."

Using both of his hands, Sam roughly yanked Morris's head back. Rachel dropped to her knees.

"No," Morris shouted.

"Don't make Ricky watch this," my father said. "Pearl will never forgive you."

Nathan exploded, running over to my father, shaking his fists. "Don't you fucking tell me what to do you piece of shit. You disloyal scumbag. I'll fucking do whatever I want and fuck Pearl too. You hear me I'll fuck her."

Nathan punched the empty cup out of my father's hands. It shattered on the floor. "I give you water to be nice and all I get from you is disrespect."

"You know Pearl," my father continued. "She's very loyal to you. But this is her son. He shouldn't be here. Shouldn't have to watch this. You know what I'm saying." Nathan didn't respond. He turned his back on my father and walked toward Rachel.

"Rachel, don't," Morris said again.

"Shut up! All of you. I've had enough of this shit."

Rachel looked sadly at her uncle. He put up his palms imploringly. Nathan lit another cigar and paced back and forth with his fly unzipped. He muttered curses. No one else made a sound. Even the Spratz brothers appeared to be afraid to move. After taking several puffs Nathan calmed down. He stopped in front of Rachel and unbuckled his belt and dropped his pants down to his ankles.

Then he turned and pointed at me. "Cover his eyes."

Larry picked up one of the rags on the floor. As he walked toward me Morris grabbed the hacksaw. Before Sam could stop him, before Rachel screamed "No!" Morris began sawing off two of his fingers.

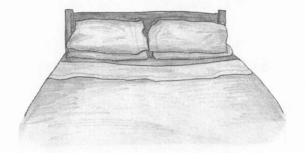

# 16.

I had never seen my father so broken. Whatever his flaws and demons, he was always an immense presence, strong and volatile. But after we returned home from the Fulton Fish Market, he turned into a withered shell. He appeared pale and fragile, wasting away in his bed. He stayed there, soiling the sheets, until the room smelled like a home for the mentally ill.

He stopped going to work and didn't take bets, so I had to keep the bookie business going. He stayed in his room and wept loudly. He wanted nobody around. Grandma was banned from the house, causing a feud. She stopped speaking to my mother. My mother went to work but when she came home she disappeared into the bedroom, slamming the door, locking me out.

My parents had placed a Do Not Disturb sign on their life. I eavesdropped whenever I could. A few nights after that terrible afternoon at the Fulton Fish Market I heard my parents talking and I got out of bed and pressed my ear against the door. I heard Nathan's name a few times, usually followed by a "fuck" or a "creep" or a threat to bring in a Jersey guy my father knew to kill him.

I went back to bed but couldn't sleep. I didn't want to,

with all the nightmares I was having, of blood shooting out of Morris's hand like a geyser, of my father tied up as Nathan cut off his fingers and toes with a scissor, of the Spratz brothers hanging my mother and me from a tree. I took out the photo album of my father in the Army. I studied the picture of my father with two other soldiers. All three had their shirts off. My father was the only one with a lot of chest hair. He looked like a beast. The other soldiers' chests were smooth and muscled. One held a sledgehammer against my father's stomach while the other grabbed his arms. They all had cigars in their mouths.

My father told me that he used to bet other soldiers that they couldn't hurt him punching him in the stomach. Was it possible? Could he really have been so strong?

Another picture showed ten soldiers forming a pyramid, my father part of the foundation. Next to it was a picture of seven soldiers holding guns dressed in jungle camouflage. My father looked the toughest, the bravest. How could that war hero be the same man now shitting in his bed? He had been through a lot, hanging from a hook, but unlike Morris he wasn't wounded. Why couldn't he get out of bed and go back to work?

With my mother and father out of commission, I knew that it was up to me to rescue the family. I sat up in bed and arranged three pillows against the headboard. Nathan. Larry. Sam.

"You have two days to get out of town," I said, staring at each pillow individually.

They laughed at me.

"Okay, now you only have one."

When I had first proposed my money-making idea to Mara

before I went to the Catskills, she was insulted and absolute in her refusal. The gypsy dances were private. I understood, and felt bad asking her again. It was wrong and could hurt our relationship. But I was convinced that it was my best chance of raising money quickly. I needed it to parlay at a craps game I'd heard about that took place in the back room of a candy store on Kingsbridge Road. I reminded her that she had said she would do anything for me. I swore her to secrecy and then described to her what Nathan and the Spratz brothers had done to my father and Morris and Rachel. I told her what they did to Nathan's best friend, Charlie Levine.

We were in her kitchen, which was even smaller than mine. There was no room for a table. The ceiling was less than six and a half feet high, with two exposed sewer pipes that jutted down another eight inches. She leaned against the refrigerator, her face ghostly.

"I don't want to," she said.

"One time. Just once."

"It's too creepy."

"It won't be. I promise."

"If anyone touches me you have to stop them."

"No one will touch you. I'll have rules."

She looked at me without speaking and let me know—her eyes pleading, her head nodding sideways—that I was making her sad. I didn't like the way that made me feel, but I said nothing. She mumbled yes and looked away.


I'd never heard my father cry before this breakdown. Now it was an everyday experience. I was in my room one night two weeks after we returned from the fish market when I heard the sound of his loud sobs.

"It's alright, Harry," my mother said. "We'll work it out. We always do."

"How?" he cried. "He wants you. That's what this is all about. I can't protect you. I don't have the money. I'm such a loser."

"No you're not. He's the loser. He's a sick fuck. That's why I chose you over him. He's shit. Nothing."

"He's still in love with you." He started crying again, louder.

My mother moaned a few times and kept repeating, "It's alright. It's alright. We'll work it out."

"I'll kill him if he touches you."

"He won't without my permission. He likes to think he's honorable."

"He's crazy. He believes he's some sort of mensch for not killing Morris. What are we going to do?"

"I'll get Suzy to ask Jeffrey again."

"Don't bother them."

"He has so much money."

"Leave them out of it!"

For several minutes neither said anything. I heard a few sobs. I climbed off my bed and tiptoed toward their room to hear better. Their door was ajar and I cautiously peaked. My father lay flat on his back, no pillow, the sheet up to his chin. My mother rested on her side above the sheet, still dressed in a skirt and blouse, her hair spread out on two pillows. She said, "I can sneak money out of Elizabeth Taylor's account. A loan. I'll pay it back."

"You'll end up in jail."

"She won't know. It's only temporary. I have it all worked out. There's so much. Nobody watches it. "

"No. I'll give him my fingers."

"I'd spend an evening with him before I would let you do that."

"Swear to me you won't."

"What's the big deal? I can close my eyes and pretend it's you."

"Swear to me."

"What if we don't have the money?"

"Swear."

"We'll get the money. Somehow."

I was having second thoughts as I stepped out of the elevator into the basement a few days later. It was like when I shoplifted those pens from Woolworth's and ended up throwing them down the sewer before I got home. But this time it was too late to change my mind. The boys were already gathering near the alley. When Mara opened the door to let me in her face was made up lightly, just some pink powder covering her acne and a little purple mascara on her eyelids. She looked beautiful, but scared.

"I'm nervous." She struggled to smile.

"You'll be great."

I went out to wait on the sidewalk with the audience. Fat Bertha looked down at me intently like she knew I was up to no good. I led the nine boys down the alley, out of her sight. Three of them were friends from my block and the others I knew from school. Behind the silver trash cans, I collected three dollars from each boy and went over the rules again. "Mara will strip off all of her clothes but you can't touch her. And not too much noise. I don't want anyone in the building to find out."

The boys ranged in age from twelve to fourteen. Most of them looked more nervous than Mara as we walked down toward the apartment. I let them in. I was about to close the door when Tony Goostaldi came running down the hall. I hadn't invited him, but Tony had a way of finding out things. He pushed me aside. I knew better than to ask him for money.

I moved the plastic Christmas tree out of the way. Most of the boys sat on the stained carpet, some on the chairs Mara had set up. They were crowded together because the room was so small. A couple of the Irish boys looked uncomfortable. I wondered if it was because of all the pictures of Jesus.

Mara had a flair for the dramatic and had sewn a costume especially for the show, made of transparent scarves and pieces of brightly colored fabric, some with sequins and glitter. It looked like a quilt or an African gown. I thought she looked glamorous and sexy. She had fixed her hair into a bun with just the sides hanging loosely. She wore green high heels.

Sparkling, she stood in front of us, waiting for the boys to be quiet. I kept shushing the boys. Mara turned on the record player and let the Hungarian gypsy music drift through the room before she began to dance. Most of the boys quieted down. Some of them shook their torsos to the music as if they were dancing. One boy I knew from school jerked his arms spastically to get laughs.

At first Mara moved slowly. Her hands floated from one side to the other like a Japanese dancer I had once seen on the Ed Sullivan show. Then her hips started to sway. The boys were beginning to make noise again, giggling at each other's antics and shouting at Mara to "take it off."

She yanked a piece of cloth off her dress. "Take it off... take it off," they chanted. Then she flung another piece to the floor. Cheers and shouts. The tempo of the music sped up. She unwound a long narrow orange scarf as she pivoted several times, exposing skin just below her breasts. Then she started to spin in the opposite direction, unwinding a red gossamer scarf. One by one she began to pull more pieces of cloths off her body. The boys groaned and giggled and hooted. They screamed with joy, jumped out of their chairs, rolled on the floor, threw their hands over their faces and peeked through their fingers. Mara teased and danced. Two boys started wrestling. Another kept pounding his fist against the floor.

Mara seemed to be enjoying herself. Maybe she felt like Marilyn Monroe, reducing men to stammering spastics. She smiled broadly and pulled a long purple scarf off her midriff. The tawny flesh of her belly rippled to the music.

She smiled at me. I smiled back, thrilled by the spectacle and excitement in the room. I watched the boys' delighted faces. I felt like an impresario—the show was a hit. I already began to think of future shows. Maybe Cynthia, the wildest girl in the neighborhood, could join in? I could charge double. I could rent the Kingsbridge Armory and make enough money to pay off Nathan, pay the Bar Mitzvah bills, move my family out of the Bronx, and send my parents on a nice trip to Nassau.

Mara took one of the boys—the smallest in the room, who clearly had not yet reached puberty, his face cherubic and freckled—and pulled him up and had him stand in front of her as she kicked off her heels and stripped off her stockings as if he she was doing this solely for him. The boy blushed a deep red and shyly hunched his shoulders and cast his eyes down to the floor, which made the other boys laugh and jeer. He sat down quickly, looking like he wanted to disappear. His friends teased him and mimicked the way he'd stood there with his shoulders rising and his hands clasped together in front of his crotch.

Mara laughed and pulled a piece of white satin off her thigh. The gypsy violins began to pulsate. She took her right hand and yanked the sequin fabric covering the top of her left breast. Mirroring that tease she stripped off the right side with her left hand, so that both of her breasts were exposed. The boys exploded with delight. One boy from school shouted, "Take it all off...everything." A neighborhood boy screamed, "Mara, let me squeeze them."

Then Tony stood up and started taking off his pants. Other boys giggled and pointed at him. The joy in Mara's face vanished and she looked at me in alarm. The audience shifted its attention to Tony, who was now holding his erection in both hands and carrying it toward Mara as if it was a gift for the Queen.

I had never seen an erection like Tony's. It was as thick as an eggplant and must have been nine inches long. Boys pushed each other, trying to back away as Tony marched through them wearing only his black sneakers and his sweaty white undershirt.

The gypsy music whirled faster, reaching a crescendo. Mara spun and jerked, her fearful eyes darting from Tony to me. I felt overwhelmed by the tension around me. My private dances with Mara had felt innocent and sweet; but the sweetness was gone now and the energy in the room was hungry and wet. Tony stepped closer until he was only a foot from Mara.

"Tony, the rules...no touching," I shouted.

My voice was swallowed in the din. Everyone was standing now, watching Tony and Mara. She stopped dancing, the concrete wall right behind her. She covered her breasts with her arms. Boys pushed forward, crowding her, jostling each other. The shorter kids in the back jumped up and down and pushed against the boys up front, thrusting their heads between bodies to see what was happening.

Mara backed up against the wall, her head flanked by pictures of Jesus. A television with a large rabbit ear antenna sat on a plastic table next to her.

Tony shoved the boys away and flailed with his elbows to make more space. He stepped forward until his erection bumped into Mara's thigh. She screamed. She started crying and looked at me for help. I hollered for Tony to stop, but he paid no attention. He grabbed her arms.

"Tony, let her go," I shouted again. I stood behind the boys watching, only a few feet away from Tony and Mara.

She pleaded with him, her tears streaming down her face. She tried to push him away but her hand seemed to excite him more. He told her to hold the huge thing.

"No!" she shouted, firmly. He put his hands on her shoulders and pressed himself against her, sandwiching her against the concrete wall.

"Just touch it and I'll let you go."

"Ricky, help me!"

Tony laughed and grabbed her breasts as his cock beat against her. "That little kike is not going to help you. Just touch it."

Mara shook her head violently. She looked like a wild animal. I was close enough to pick up a chair and hit Tony over the head. I wanted to gather some boys and charge him.

I glanced around the room, but nobody looked like they were willing to mess with him. Two boys knocked over chairs in their scramble to get out the door. Others stayed, watching. I stepped a foot closer, within arm's reach of pulling Tony away from her.

"Leave her alone!" I shouted.

"You got nice titties," Tony said. He handled them. He squeezed them.

"Let me go," she said, trying to pry his hands off.

"What's the magic word?"

"Please, please Tony."

"Wrong. Just touch it."

"No!" Mara screamed and thrust her knee into his balls. She broke free and ran to the bathroom. Tony quickly recovered and chased after her, his bouncing erection leading the way.

She slammed the door and I heard the lock click.

"Open the door you cock-teaser!" He banged with his fist.

"Tony," I yelled, "You better get dressed and go. Her father will be home any minute and he's got a gun."

Boys stumbled over each other to escape from the room. Only a couple of boys remained besides Tony and me. He turned my way. His hand moved up and down on his cock. He pointed it in my direction. "You touch it."

"You better go. Her father has a bad temper."

"So do I."

He marched, cock in hand, toward me. As I backed up, I bashed my head on a foot-long copper crucifix hanging on the wall. I put up my hand to feel the cut, and he thrust his erection against my crotch. "Touch it or I'm going to kick your ass."

"Come on, Tony, I thought we were friends. Let me go. My

head's bleeding."

He punched me in the stomach. As I doubled over, he rubbed that thing against my face. Mara sobbed loudly in the bathroom.

"Touch it. Now! Or I'll make you suck it."

So I touched it for a second with two fingers. It felt slimy. Tony moaned and slapped me hard in the face.

"You queer. Now suck it."

"No. Come on Tony, don't. You said—"

"Suck it." He grabbed my neck and squeezed. Then he stuck his cock in my mouth and I gagged. I dropped to the floor, on my hands and knees. I felt like vomiting.

"You queer," he said, again, slapping me in the head. "Lick it once and I'll let you go."

I crawled away from him. No longer thinking straight, I stayed down, like a dog with his tail between his legs. When he caught me he pulled up my head by my ears. "Lick it."

It was bouncing against my lips, covered with a mist from my breath and mouth. I put out the tip of my tongue and licked his cock from the bottom to the top and breathed in his moldy cheese smell and tasted his stale piss.

Tony moaned, breathing hard. He slapped me again, called me a queer again, and ordered me to lick it one more time. My head hung down, my mouth open, trying to catch my breath. The last remaining boys opened the door and ran out.

I shook my head. He stood over me as if he was urinating and clamped both of his hands on my head, lifting it up, drawing it toward his cock. Then he let go and smashed my temples with the sides of his fists. My head felt like it spit in half and the vomit poured out of me.

He backed away, but still got splatter on his sneakers. He wiped them on my shirt and pants. Then he kicked me down into the vomit.

"Hey faggot, tell your girlfriend I'm coming back." He pulled on his boxer shorts and pants and left.

I lay crying. In the bathroom Mara moaned. I crawled over to the closed bathroom door and apologized to her. "Please come out. He's gone. Please forgive me."

"Go way," she shouted from behind the door. "Why didn't you help me? You let him do that to me. You're just like him. Get out!"

"Mara, I'm sorry." I started to cry again. Not only for her, but for my cowardice. Why didn't I help her sooner? Why didn't I punch Tony in the stomach? Or pick up a chair and smash him? "Please don't be mad at me. Please. He attacked me too. You can have all the money."

"Just leave me alone and never come back down here."

"Don't say that."

I sat for awhile, hunched over crying. I tried the knob again but it was locked.

"Mara, please open the door."

"Go way."

The needle was stuck on the record, making a repetitive whining sound, so I stood up and lifted the arm and shut off the record player. I found paper towels and cleaned up the vomit, but the stain and the smell remained. I moved the fake Christmas tree back into the center of the room, righted the fallen chairs, and placed all the money on the table. Then I left.

# 17.

I didn't want to leave the house, didn't want to see my friends and hear the taunts: queer, fag, coward, chickenshit. While my father wasted away in his bed, I brooded in mine, calling myself all the ugly names I didn't want my friends to call me. The map of the world was spread across the wall above me and I searched for countries to run away to. I had cousins in Israel. I could go to Hungary with Mara if she would forgive me. Or maybe China, like my father. Anywhere but here in the Bronx, where I would have to see my friends, and bump into Tony again.

That night, after the awful scene in Mara's apartment, I listened to my Haftorah on the record player. The rabbi's gravelly voice chanted Hebrew, the waitress shouted orders in the background, and the static of the cheap recording cackled. The Bar Mitzvah was fast approaching. It was going to be a disaster. What was the point of becoming a man? I had already blown it. I was a cocksucker.

I couldn't concentrate on Hebrew. I was terrified that Tony would ambush me again or come back after Mara again like he said he would. I revisited each step. Tony running down the hall, entering the house, stripping off his clothes, bumping into Mara, turning on me, sticking his cock into my mouth, making me lick it.

"No, no," I cried, cringing when I thought of what I'd done. Yet I felt compelled to keep reliving it. I stuck out my tongue and licked the air. His odor filled the room as if he was there.

"No," I said out loud, but kept licking, trying to erase the image from my system through sheer repetition.

I tightened my stomach and punched myself. I stood a pillow on my abdomen and pretended it was Tony. I smashed him into bits. I was a man's man like those toy soldiers looking down at me, like those men with rifles and bayonets in my father's war album.

After awhile I got out of bed and closed the venetian blinds. Then I pulled down my pajama bottoms so they curled around my ankles. I took a fat pillow and rolled on top of it, humping it as I imagined Marilyn Monroe, assuring myself that I was a ladies' man too.

When my mother knocked on the door I pulled up my pajamas, turned over, and used the pillow to hide my erection. She came in and sat down on the edge of the bed. I shut off the record player and slid over to give her room. "You feeling okay?" she asked.

"Sure. Just tired."

"Something is bothering you."

"Nothing." No way was I going to confide to her or anyone about what had happened. I shared too much with her already. I saw the way she controlled Suzy's life. The way Grandma tried to control her life. I wouldn't allow that to happen to me. I felt myself tightening, like Harry Houdini strapped in a straitjacket, and like that great escape artist, I needed to break free.

"How's the speech coming?"

"It's going to be a flop."

"Don't worry, it's like a Broadway show. The rehearsals, even the night before, are often terrible, but on opening night it all comes together. You'll be great. The show will be a hit."

"Well, I wouldn't invest any money it," I said, making her smile.

"Don't let our money problems make you unhappy. Pretty soon Nathan will be paid off and we'll get back to our normal lives."

"Where we going to get the money?"

"Maybe I'll take your advice and ask Marilyn Monroe for a loan."

"I heard you talking to Daddy about stealing some money from Elizabeth Taylor's account."

She looked down at me. "Just borrowing...for a little while."

"You once told me that your boss trusted you. He knew you wouldn't ever betray that trust."

"Maybe he's taking advantage of me."

"Mom, don't steal. This isn't shoplifting."

She closed her eyes, but the tears sneaked out and slid down her cheeks. "Sometimes to help someone you have to do something you don't want to do."

"I'm going to have a lot of money when I grow up. I don't

want these problems."

"It's not just having money. It's knowing how to use it. All of our clients have money. They're still not happy. Jeffrey and Suzy have money. They're miserable, just like Jeffrey's parents. It all comes down to family. How you were raised."

The tears came faster now and she shook her head as if apologizing for crying. I grabbed her hands and rubbed her knuckles. I could hear Fat Bertha shouting at someone, telling him not to park in front of the Chinese laundry.

"I thought she would learn to love Jeffrey. He would take care of her. I didn't want her to have my money problems."

Her head sank lower and she began to shake. I grabbed her around the back of her neck and hugged her and rubbed her shoulders and her scalp.

"You're always there for me," she said. "My little companion."

I looked up at the two hundred toy soldiers on the shelves above my bed, some with rifles, others riding in tanks. Several had bayonets on their muzzles ready to strike. I glanced at Spain, where Christopher Columbus set sail. I could go there, make a new start.

"After my Bar Mitzvah things will change. I have to make my own life."

"We can still be close."

"Sometimes I feel we're too close."

She flinched and lifted her head. She ran a hand though my hair. As if I was already breaking away, a look of bitterness passed over her face. She camouflaged it quickly with a knowing smile.

"All I'm saying is that when I'm grown up I won't be here.

I'll have my own life."

"Good. Goodbye. Good riddance."

She shut down as she sat up. I knew this pose well. Now it was she who was gazing at the map of the world. She had never traveled. Except for one trip to Las Vegas, visiting Suzy in Philadelphia and relatives in Baltimore was as far from the Bronx as she'd ever gone. Her silence took over the room. I thought she was about to leave when she turned and stroked my hair and forehead and began to sing a song that she had written for the movie *I'll Cry Tomorrow*. Unfortunately, she had delivered it a week late. The producers had already bought a theme song from Johnny Mercer.

*I'll cry tomorrow, just tonight be mine.*
*I'll sigh tomorrow, make tonight divine...*
*For too soon it's over*
*And I know that you'll be gone...*

It didn't take much for me to fall under her spell. My resolve to resist her, to break away from her control, crumbled beneath the power of her minor keys. Did she know what she was doing? It's hard to say. Like any snake charmer she played chords that could hypnotize.

*Taking your magic,*
*Just my tears will linger on.*
*I'll cry tomorrow,*
*I'll gladly cry tomorrow,*
*Just say you're mine tonight.*

When she finished singing, she gazed down at me with her hand on my chest. Her look was so sad, as if I was the one good thing in her life, as if she might go to prison for embezzlement and her only chance of surviving was knowing I would be there when she got out. I reached up again to pull her toward me, but she resisted a little. I pressed harder, clasping my hands together. Then she let go and collapsed on top of me. Her head rested on my chest. Her thick black hair tickled my face. We spoke of many things: Suzy and Jeffrey, old boyfriends, her feud with Grandma, her memories of her father, Marilyn Monroe, Richard Burton and Elizabeth Taylor, why she stayed with my father, who was coming to my Bar Mitzvah and how much money they would give me, how Elizabeth Taylor was so rich that twenty thousand dollars to her was like twenty cents to us. The cost of two black cherry sodas, that's all, not a big deal.

I didn't tell her what happened with Mara and Tony. I spoke instead of other schemes I had for making money. She quickly found the flaws in all of them. But while she critiqued my ideas she stroked my arm. There was not even a hint of arousal in the intimacy between my mother and me. But I was aware that when we lay together like this and talked of our lives, we were more like husband and wife than mother and child.

When the phone rang, it startled me—who could be calling so late? My mother was still up and she answered it in the kitchen. I carefully lifted the receiver on my bedroom phone, my hand covering the voice box, and heard Nathan say, "Charlie's dead."

"What happened?" my mother asked.

"Fell off the roof of the Golden Nugget hotel," Nathan said. "I miss him already."

"He was a terrific guy. A lot of good memories."

"Those were great days. We should have made up. Now it's too late."

"The two of you were too proud."

Nathan didn't respond for what seemed like a long time. My mother breathed heavily into the telephone. I knew she hated him for what he had done to my father. When Nathan finally spoke again his words came haltingly. "Pearl, listen to me. You're not going to raise the money. Why kill yourself? We've all suffered enough. I've never stopped loving you. You know that. Without Charlie, now it's all so clear. You're all I have from my past. I'm not asking you to leave Harry. I just want one night with you. One night to give me some pleasure. That's not a lot to ask. Not for all I've done for you."

"I can't. The memories of you and Charlie, I think of them often. Those days were the best. But life moves on. We can't go back."

"One night. Just you and me. Like the old days. What's the crime? You should do it out of loyalty to me. As a friend. Forget the forgiveness on the money. I'm just throwing that in. I need you now with Charlie gone."

The silence returned. My heart raced. She should just hang up. Even if she's scared she should tell him to go fuck himself. I looked out the window at the empty train tracks bending toward Mosholou. Joe's was closed. No one was on the sidewalk. The lights of a car streamed by.

"I'm old fashioned," she said. "When I was thirteen, I heard my mother cry like I had never heard. It sounded like ripping, stitches being pulled from her heart, one after another. I ran to her room, 'Mom, what is it, what's wrong?' She just kept shrieking. I climbed into her bed and held my mother in my arms as if I was the mother. My father wasn't there. He was away with another woman. My mother had just found out. You can't ask me to do this."

"All I do is give. When do I get? You won't do this for me, okay, then I want my money, all of it."

"You'll get it. I just need a month's extension. The Bar Mitzvah is taking up a lot of my time with all the planning. Give us till Yom Kippur."

"What do I get?"

"Vigorish. We'll pay you another $500."

"No!" Nathan shouted. "I'm tired of being a schmuck. You want an extra month, I want you in my bed. That's the deal."

When my mother spoke again I heard the fear in her voice even though she was making a joke. "On Yom Kippur you're going to commit adultery?"

"Why not?" Nathan said. "Then I can atone for my sins."

My mother chuckled tightly. "I forgot how funny you can be."

"Sometimes I wonder if Harry hadn't come back from the war, would we have gotten together?"

"Who knows? Who would have thought I'd be borrowing money from skinny Nat who was always hitting me up for a nickel or a dime."

"That's why I'm so soft around you. You never turned me down. Even if you had to hock a necklace, you always helped me out."

"So Nathan, be a mensch. Give me to Yom Kippur."

"Five thousand extra in interest. If I don't get all my money when I'm done fasting you spend the weekend with me."

"You'll get your money."

"You're all I have from the past."

"We'll always be friends."

Nathan coughed. Then he said, "I'm a pussycat, but if someone screws me, like your fucking husband did, I screw them back. I fuck them over. And their wives. And their children. And their grandchildren."

"Nathan, please calm down. Nathan, this is your friend, Pearl. Please. The debt will be paid...one way or the other."

"Good," he said, trying to clear his throat. "I hate when I get aggravated at you. It kills me. I'm on edge with Charlie's death. I'm alone. It's lonely here."

"I know."

After she hung up, my mother stopped at my room. "He's crazy," she said. "I can't talk now. We'll talk in the morning. Don't be afraid. It will all work out."

"You sounded scared."

"Nathan can be scary. But he won't harm me or you." She said this, but her hands were shaking.

"How are you going to get the money?"

"I can't talk now." She walked out of the room.

I wondered how crazy Nathan was. He had personally sawed off almost half of Charlie's arm. Threatened my mother. Hung my father on a hook. How could he think she still loved him? How could she have ever loved him? And what did it say about my mother that her two best childhood friends became gangsters, that she married a bookie and small-time crook, that she still shoplifted, and was planning on stealing money from Elizabeth Taylor?

I smelled her on my sheets, her perfume and sweat. Nathan's slug-like tongue filled my mind. His smirk and cold voice. Fear traveled down my spine and into my gut as I thought about killing him. I turned the record player back on, wanting to distract myself. The droning of the rabbi chanting was calming, though I couldn't remember a single Hebrew sentence. Maybe I would cancel the Bar Mitzvah and never become a man. I would stay a boy, living with my mother, allowing her to dictate my life and sing me to sleep.

With new resolve, I played the record over and over again, concentrating hard. I had to become a man, had to protect my mother from Nathan. Had to get the money somehow. This time I wouldn't chicken out. But after I rescued my family, I was determined to move out of my mother's gravitational field. She was too powerful and had too much influence over me. I looked again at the map. Argentina, Bolivia, Greece. Maybe Poland, I probably still had some distant cousins there.

Suzy, over a hundred miles away, was still under my mother's control. It wasn't enough to leave home, marry, and live in another city. Suzy proved that. Pearl's fingerprints were all over Suzy's life. Even immigrating to another continent might not take me beyond my mother's reach. Her songs could ride on radio waves and hunt me down anywhere on earth.

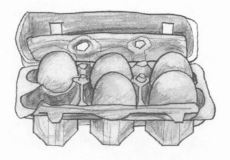

# 18.

The next time the phone rang again, it was morning. I had overslept. I reached for my pad and pencil, but it wasn't a bettor. It was Grandma.

"Hello Rickalah, how are you?"

"Good. I miss you."

"I miss you, my kinder. Is the house falling apart without me?"

"The whole building is beginning to collapse." I looked out the window as I said this and saw Fat Bertha watching me. Did she know about Tony?

"Ha, ha. How's Pearl? Don't tell her I called."

"I don't see her much. She's busy at work and taking care of Daddy."

"You memorize your Haftorah?"

"Working on it."

"Why don't you come visit me?"

"I will. I've been busy. Daddy's not answering the phone so I have to take all the bets."

She muttered some Yiddish, which I was sure were curses or insults. Then she said, "Alright, kindalah, be good to your mother. Call me."

"Okay, Grandma. I'll come visit, soon."

After I hung up and ate breakfast, I went back to my room and set pillows on the bed to create an audience for my Bar Mitzvah speech. I turned on the record player and placed the needle on the groove. The rabbi's hoarse voice chanted Hebrew words. After listening several times, I shut off the player to see how I would do without it. I smiled at the pillows and waved to friends and family. I went to the window and saw my real friends playing stickball. I hadn't been outside since the gypsy dance three days ago and I still wasn't ready to face them. What if Tony showed up? Would Fat Bertha protect me? She was looking at me again from across the way. The heavy bags under her eyes seemed thicker than usual, as if they were weighted with sand. As if she knew what had happened and her pity for me weighed her down.

I began trying to recite my Haftorah but my mind was a total blank. Not one Hebrew word broke through the fog. Like a boxer knocked out on his feet I leaned one way, then the other, then staggered around the room, finally falling on the bed, down for the count. I slapped my hand on the bed several times, as if it was a canvas floor, and I was the referee as well as the defeated fighter. I was going to give the worst Bar Mitzvah speech in recorded history. I would be forever known as that pitiful anemic boy who licked Tony's gigantic cock, got beaten up by girls, mangled his Bar Mitzvah speech, disgraced his parents, embarrassed the Jews, and dynamited the bridge to manhood.

My father was slowly coming out of his funk and talked about returning to work. He started taking bets again and about a week after Grandma called I visited her. She had been alone in her apartment now for three weeks. The bus to her building was a slow, fumy ride. As the bus moved passed 170th Street into the lower Bronx, blacks and Hispanics filled the sidewalk. Grandma was one of only a few white people left in her building. The exodus had started a few years back. Some black families moved in, some white families moved to Westchester or Long Island. Old whites died, young blacks came. White doctors fled the neighborhood. Some Spanish-speaking people moved in. The migration accelerated.

As I got off the bus I thought of how to persuade my grandmother to come back to our apartment. I could tell her how much I missed her cooking. How I missed our afternoon snacks together: Yankee Doodle cupcakes and chocolate milk.

I rode the elevator up and banged on her door. "Grandma! It's me, Ricky!" It took a while for her to come. One of her neighbors down the hall, a Puerto Rican woman with long blond hair, opened her door, looked at me, and waved before closing it again. Grandma's neighbors were mostly Hispanic. The couple next door had told me that they liked her so they tolerated her loud TV. Grandma said her neighbors always helped her to open pickle jars and thread needles.

"Is that you, Rickalah?"

"Yes, Grandma, it's me."

As she unlocked her three locks, a blast of heat hit me. I never understood why the steam pipes in her apartment, which were exposed along the back wall and under the ceiling, were always on, even during the summer.

She looked so happy to see me. I waited in the kitchen as

she finished making up her face. Her two windows faced an interior courtyard where the sun never shone. Cockroaches crawled along her walls. The ceilings were peeling several layers of lead paint. She tried to liven up the place with doilies on the kitchen table and coffee table, and quilts and throws draped over the torn couch and upholstered chair. Framed pictures of her parents and cousins, and herself as a young girl riding a pony, hung on the wall above her bed. The smell of mildew and old paint and old cupboards and old bodies and old garbage saturated the apartment.

We sat at her kitchen table and drank iced tea while she told stories of her youth, most of which I'd heard many times before. As a nine-year-old child she had emigrated alone from Poland. She remembered the waves crashing against the ship and crying herself to sleep at night in her cabin. When she arrived in New York, she lived in a tenement on the lower east side with her two brothers and their wives and children. There was no hot water and no toilet in the apartment.

She married Abe at sixteen, happy to get out of there. He was a prince, she said, born in America, educated, handsome, so high class. He sold Valentine boxes to candy companies and made a decent living, but he had to travel a lot. When the children came, first George, then Pearl, Rosie was often alone with them for weeks at a time.

He died of a heart attack right before the Depression, and she was forced to move with her two teenage children to this $30 a month rent-controlled apartment. Her children helped her out then. George dropped out of school and worked in the garment center and gave her money. Pearl always split any money she earned singing in the mountains. Even after George moved to Manhattan, he checked on her every day. "If he had lived, he never would've allowed Pearl to do this to me," she said, looking bitter.

She told me about the horror of receiving the telegram—*The Secretary of War desires me to express his deepest regret that your son Private George Simon was killed in action on twenty two November, 1942, in Italy*—while she was playing poker with friends in her apartment. All of those friends were now dead. She cried and held her hands to her heart and said, "It aches."

Left with little money after Abe died, and no work experience, she managed to get by working as a seamstress for friends and neighbors, but she never got over Abe's infidelity. After she found out, she cursed him every day until he died and then she cursed him for dying and leaving her almost penniless.

She had always liked men, liked the attention, liked dolling up and being courted. During her widow years, she usually had a boyfriend, but Abe's infidelity had killed something inside her and she was never able again to lose herself to love, except for her family. "That's why I sacrifice everything for you, my kindalah. And Pearl doesn't even call me. Throws me out like a bum."

"Daddy is feeling better. I'm sure Mom will call you now."

"For what, for what, to end up alone in this cockroach apartment, unappreciated? Mr. Fein couldn't come over today because he had to take his daughter to the doctor. So he said. He's a weasel, probably out with other women. No time for me, but taking good care of himself."

Later in the afternoon she sat watching *The Edge of Night* while I lay on the sofa thinking about her life. Emigrating from

Poland, World War I and World War II and the Depression, the deaths of her husband and son and brothers and cousins and friends, and no money, and now she'd been alone for weeks in her hot apartment. Her loneliness seeped through her skin and settled into the sofa, the chair, the bed. I felt it wherever I sat, wherever I stood. I imagined her sitting by the phone, day after day, waiting for it to ring, waiting for Pearl to beg her to come back.

The judge on the TV screen was also home alone, recovering from an auto accident. His head was bandaged and his arm in a sling. He was tall and handsome but he looked worried. He picked up the telephone, looked at it and slammed it down.

The judge let a woman into his house. They sat down on a couch and talked and held hands. She wasn't his wife. Grandma adjusted her glasses and peered closer. The volume hurt my ears so I covered them with my hands. The woman showed the judge some medals, which he took from her and examined.

"He'd be furious with Pearl," Grandma told the judge as if she was still talking to me. "George would tell her 'Who cares what that no good bum lying in bed wants, that bulvan, that momzer, that pig.'" She spit on the rug. "'You have to respect your mother and never ever again treat her like this. Not after all she has done for you, sacrificing herself, cooking, cleaning, taking care of your children, not moving to Miami because you needed her, never asking for a penny, and then you throw her away like a dish rag.'" She nodded as if agreeing with her dead son and wiped away tears with her handkerchief.

"No," Grandma said to the judge, thrusting her finger toward her chest. "Never. Pearl has to call me. Why should I call her? Pearl should call me." The judge looked bewildered. He rose from the couch and combed through documents on his desk with his one good hand. He slapped the desk and then swiped at the documents, knocking them to the floor. The woman rushed over and hugged him.

Grandma cried. Her large sagging breasts heaved as her shoulders shook. She couldn't catch her breath.

"Are you alright, Grandma?" I said.

"Rickalah, you're still here?"

"Yes, I'm right here on the sofa."

She turned her head in my direction. "You have to help me. I don't know what is happening."

"What's wrong? Is it your breathing?"

"Ricky, huh-huh-huh," she panted. She looked terrified, and I was afraid that she might be having a heart attack. "I don't know why the judge is—huh-huh. I don't know who that woman is. I don't understand what's going on."

"Grandma, turn down the television so I can hear you."

"I don't know...I don't know what's happening...I don't know what's wrong with me." She lowered herself to the floor the way she did when she was fighting with my mother and banging her head against the bed. Only this time, there was no banging, just wailing and panting. She covered her face with her arms.

"It's okay, Grandma." I walked over and turned down the volume, then sat down beside her and patted her shoulders. "Tell me what you think is happening."

She continued panting and moaning so it took awhile for me to understand what she was saying. She told me about the car accident, the woman, the lawyers who looked at the judge strangely, and his children who showed him pictures of his family. I stroked her head and neck, laughing. "It's okay. You're okay." I turned the volume back up to make sure I was right.

"The judge has amnesia from the car accident," I said. "He doesn't know who he is. It's confusing. That's why you don't understand. There's nothing wrong with you."

"But he was holding hands with that other woman."

"She's a nurse. She's just trying to help him get back his memory."

Her crying quieted. She chuckled in between her sobs. "Rickalah, thank you, thank you. Mmmwha! Mmmwha!" She kissed my hand several times. "I thought maybe I was going senile."

"I know. It's okay. You're so smart Grandma, you don't have to worry." I helped her up. She sat back in her chair.

"I miss you."

"I miss you, too. You'll be back at our house soon, after the Bar Mitzvah."

"Are you ready?"

"No."

"I don't know if I want to come back."

"Of course you do; we need you."

"Now you need me? What about last month?"

"Last month we needed you also. But Daddy was too crazy."

She dried her face with her hands and took off her glasses and rubbed her eyes. "Pearl has to call me first."

"Okay, Grandma. Let's go do the shopping."


I was glad to get out of there when we went to the store.

My stomach turned a loop as the elevator dropped down quickly. I felt guilty. I should've visited her sooner. Should've called more.

We strolled arm in arm down the street filled with aromas of overripe melons and pickled fish. The sidewalk bustled with women shopping, squeezing pears and plums at the fruit stand and putting them back, peering into the window of the butcher shop at the meats hanging from hooks. Faded Hebrew letters were still stenciled on to the glass, though it no longer was a kosher butcher.

"I need to talk to you," Grandma said, stopping in front of a rusted-out Pontiac. I sat on the hood, my legs dangling off the side. She slipped a hand into her purse and took out a large white egg. "I told your mother twenty-five years ago not to marry your father. He was a bum. She didn't listen. You listen to me. I know you need me. He needs my help. Him I don't care about, but your mother and you, you need me. Take this egg and hide it in your pants. You go in the store ahead of me and walk over to the dairy section where the eggs are. You drop the egg on the floor. Fershtay my kinder? You understand?"

"How is that going to help?" I dreaded the answer.

"I thought you were so smart." She leaned against the car. The sun beating on the hood made the metal extremely hot. I couldn't put my bare hands down so I rested them on my lap. "I'm going to sue the supermarket."

"You can't do that. It's not right."

"What a stupid boy. You think the supermarket cares about me?"

"You might get hurt. Even if you get some money, it wouldn't be for years."

"You're a young boy, you don't know. With me they settle right away."

"Rosie," an old woman about the same size as Grandma shouted as she came up to us.

"What?" Grandma shouted back. She slipped the egg back in her purse.

"You don't hear me?"

"I hear you."

"It's me, Clara. You don't recognize me?"

"Of course I know it's you. There's so many crazy people on the street. You have to be careful."

"I didn't want to tell you. You remember Mr. Sullivan?"

"He owned the hardware store."

"You don't see so good and you don't hear so good, but you got a good memory. He was hit by a car. Puerto Ricans. His wife was looking out the window and saw him fly fifty feet in the air."

"Terrible news."

"I heard about Mrs. Finkle. Heart attack on the subway. They had to stop all the trains."

Grandma put up both her arms and hugged Clara. "Terrible. Terrible news."

After they separated Clara asked, "You got someone to replace her in your poker game?"

"Yeah, plenty old people begging to get in."

"I wouldn't mind playing," Clara said. "There aren't many games left anymore."

Grandma turned her head to look at me with a hint of a smile on her face. With her free hand she rubbed my thigh. I knew it was a signal, a conspiratorial wink. She was always bragging how everybody wanted her to play in their poker games. ("Play with us, Mrs. Simon. A little poker?") She said she was in demand because she was such a good person and such a good player. I didn't think it ever dawned on her that maybe the reason she was so popular was because she was almost *blind* and could barely see the numbers and suits on the cards. She always *lost*. ("A little poker, Mrs. Simon? We'll make room for you.")

"Bye bye, Clara."

"Rosie, don't forget, I'd like to play in that game."

"Bye bye."

Grandma combed her hair with her hand and for a second her hand moved toward Clara's head as if she was comparing who was taller.

We walked another block and she stopped again in front of the supermarket. She peered into her compact mirror. She applied red lipstick and smeared rouge on her cheeks.

"She shrunk. She used to be taller than me. I'm taller now, aren't I?"

"Yes, Grandma, you're bigger."

She looked from side to side to see if anyone was watching. She stuck her hand in her pocketbook and tried to hand me the egg like a spy passing documents. "Make sure no one is looking."

"I won't do it," I whispered, pushing the egg away.

"Don't be a baby."

"I won't. You might get hurt."

"I am hurt." She forced the egg into my hand. "We're all hurt."

I held it and thought about Nathan and how nice it would

be to have the money. His sneer was still vivid in my mind. And the way he threatened my mother on the telephone.

Special prices on milk and tuna fish were posted on the glass storefront. As I slipped the egg into my pocket, Grandma told me where to stand, how far from the egg cartons. Then she strode into the supermarket. I followed. She walked down the aisle and waited by the bread shelves in front of the Silvercups and Wonderbreads.

For a second, my stomach clamped so tight that I couldn't breathe or hear the clatter of shopping carts. The florescent lights seemed to shine on me like a spotlight. My fingers toyed with the egg. The shell felt fragile. I was afraid it would break in my hand. I knew what I was about to do was wrong.

I walked toward the refrigerated products and stood three feet from the dairy case, as Grandma had directed. I slid the egg out of my pocket. When no one was around I opened my hand and let it drop and quickly walked away to the end of the aisle, where I lingered, waiting to see what would happen.

Several shoppers passed by. An old black man with curly gray hair pointed and shouted to a woman to be careful of the mess on the floor. That was the cue Grandma no doubt had been hoping for. She picked up two loaves of white bread and marched forward, never hesitating.

I assumed she was going to pretend to slip, but that didn't seem to be her plan. She strode toward the egg as though it wasn't there. Her will must've erased it from her mind. So when she slipped, she truly slipped, falling backward, her feet flying in the air, her old bones crashing to the floor with a cracking thud. Her only cushion was the bread, which she managed to drop beneath her back.

It happened so fast. She was walking. Next, was in the air, almost horizontal, like a person being levitated by a magician. Then she was moaning on the ground. She was crazy and I was her accomplice. My mother would not forgive this. She was going to kill me.

"God help me," Grandma cried.

She lay, not moving, on the silver linoleum. I ran over and so did other shoppers.

Her glasses had fallen off and her eyes, covered by cataracts, looked like chipped marbles. "My back, the pain," Grandma said, in a weak voice. "Am I bleeding?"

A crowd formed a circle around her. They offered consoling advice. The nervous white store manager came running over. He had a thin mustache and was almost chinless, his lower lip covering whatever bone was there. "Are you alright?" he asked, kneeling down.

"Don't cross-examine her now," a heavy black woman shouted, as if Grandma had planted her there. "Get an ambulance."

"Get an ambulance," another shopper repeated.

"Let her be," a tall man said, placing his large hand on the manager's shoulder.

I paced nearby. Grandma hadn't filled me in on the rest of the plan.

"Should I call a doctor?" the manager asked her.

"Yes, get an ambulance quick," Grandma said, loud enough for the shoppers to hear. Tears poured from her eyes wetting the surplus powder on her cheeks. She had fallen several times before—on sidewalks, getting off buses, in other stores, sometimes by accident, other times on purpose—and had lain on her back, looking up at the faces in the crowd. I knew that, but it didn't make me feel better. "Why can't I breathe?" She asked. "My chest, it collapsed." I couldn't tell if she was for real or if this was part of the scam.

"Will she be alright?" the store manager asked the black paramedic.

"She looks pretty bad." He concentrated on his work, talking to Grandma, taking her vital signs, placing a stretcher beside her, and lifting her up onto it with the help of his partner. The manager pointed to Grandma's feet. "It wasn't our fault. Her shoes are broken." Both of her heels were loose and the sole was coming apart on one of the shoes.

"Save it for the courtroom," the paramedic said.

They wheeled Grandma out of the store. Several people in the crowd nodded and smiled at me. Some offered words of good luck and encouragement in English and Spanish. The two black men slid her into the ambulance outside. One of them gave me a hand and I climbed in.

As I watched the paramedic attend to my grandmother, I thought about her dying. She rarely was sick and was still strong enough to carry two bundles of groceries for several blocks when she couldn't find a shopping cart to steal. Except for her falls, she never went to the hospital. Her mind was sharp. However, her hearing and eyesight were both getting worse, and recently she had gone to see the doctor for pains around her liver.

"Hiya doll," the paramedic said, gently. "You okay?"

"Yeah, my back hurts, but I'm fine."

His skin was a cocoa color. He spoke with a Caribbean accent. Even when he wasn't smiling he looked as if he was having a private little laugh. Grandma lay gazing up at the oxygen tank and his handsome face. He held her hand in his large hands as he knelt beside her. He told her he remembered her from three years earlier, when he had found her lying on the sidewalk in front of an eight-story building, having slipped on a melting Good Humor bar. She couldn't sue Good Humor, though she had tried, but she did get nine hundred dollars from the building's landlord. She brushed her palm along the paramedic's white covered thigh.

"You really had them this time. The store manager, I thought his lips were going to fall off. I want a percentage. I figure I put on a good act for you out there." He winked at me. The driver, who was chuckling in the mirror, leaned his head back, his round cheeks swelling.

"Thank you, but my back could be broken."

"If I go to court," the paramedic said, in a serious voice, "and tell them this is the second time I've picked you up off the ground, you won't get a dime. And they'll believe me. I still have the Good Humor stick."

The driver and the paramedic looked at each other in the mirror and laughed.

"I'll tell the judge that I was pregnant," Grandma said, looking up fondly at the paramedic, "and I lost the baby because you knocked that tank on my stomach."

He leaned in close to her. "And I'll tell your boyfriend that I was the father of the baby."

Grandma laughed, grabbing his arm. "Ha ah ah you very smart. I'll give you ten percent."

"Keep it doll. Buy yourself a trip to Miami."

"I'd like to go but my boyfriend, Mr Fein, he's so cheap, a real piker, he won't spend the money."

"I'll take you."

"You? Feh! They don't like schwarzes in the south."

"They like them in New York?" The paramedic asked, imitating her accent. He winked at me again. I winked back. I felt much calmer. Grandma seemed okay.

"Sure. Pearl has a schwarze who cleans the house once a month. She gives the schwarze everything. I clean the house beautifully. There's nothing to do. Pearl steals my social security to give the schwarze extra money. The schwarze says she likes a blouse, Pearl gives it to her. Maybe I fix you up with the schwarze, a very nice girl."

"Why don't you fix me up with this Pearl; I could use a new shirt." Grandma didn't seem to get the joke at first, but when she did, she laughed giddily. She looked at his beaming face and she closed her eyes.

With her eyes closed, however, and her breathing labored, she looked older than her laughter. Her make-up was a mess. Her eighty-four years of life, at times disguised by her energy and will, were fully exposed as she lay still on the stretcher. She looked like the old sick people I'd seen at the hospitals when I went for blood tests.

The paramedic glanced at me, still smiling. But when he turned his gaze back to Grandma and felt her pulse with his long brown fingers against her powdery neck, he couldn't hide his concern.

# 19.

Grandma was in the hospital with a broken pelvis and was going to miss my Bar Mitzvah. I didn't tell my mother about my role in the fall. Grandma promised that she wouldn't either. If we ever collected settlement money from the supermarket's insurance company, then I might mention that I was her accomplice.

My father had returned to work. A week before my Bar Mitzvah he and I had a talk. A real talk, like one I would have with my mom. I didn't know if she had put him up to it, or if this was one of the rituals of being Bar Mitzvah, something Jewish boys had been sharing with their fathers for thousands of years. The conversation was certainly forced at first. Talking wasn't something that we did. He was my father, not my friend or confidant. We played sports together. We reviewed the daily wagers together. Sometimes we ate dinner together and sometimes we would lie together watching television or talking about the Giants or Yankees. He would often put his hand on my thigh as I lay beside him. He had a distinct scent, a little gamey, but I liked it. This was the nature of our intimacy, watching TV together, his hand connecting us, his smell filtering through me.

One thing we never did was talk about feelings. This time was different. The television was off. My mother was at an opening of a play. The night air felt cooler than it had all summer. I lay beside him on clean sheets on the bed that had been his home during his breakdown.

"So in a couple of weeks, you'll be a man. Do you know what that means?"

I didn't know what to say. I nodded.

"A lot of things change. Your responsibilities are different."

"Like what?"

"Don't be a wise guy. They're different. You'll see."

"Okay."

"How you act with girls is different."

"I know what sex is if that's what you're…"

"You don't know what sex is. You only think you do from gutter talk. Sex is everything. Remember that."

What? I didn't know how to respond or what that meant, but it felt important, like a secret, an initiation into a men's club. Perhaps this was the real Bar Mitzvah.

"Everything. I wish my father had told me that. I would have done things differently."

"Like what?"

"I said don't be a wise guy."

"I'm not. I just want to know what you would've done differently."

"This is between us. Nothing gets repeated to your mother."

"Scout's honor," I said, raising my pinkie. He ignored the gesture.

"I wouldn't have gotten married so soon. Would have played around more. That stuff they teach you about being married before you have sex, don't believe it. You want to have sex first. Make sure it's good. You have to be careful. Always use a rubber. Try a lot of girls. Make sure the one you marry is the right one. Not a faker."

"What do you mean?"

"Some girls fake it. They're frigid."

Once he seemed to find his talking rhythm and got past the awkwardness, he didn't stop for over an hour. Besides sex and the Bar Mitzvah, and being a man, and fighting in the Philippines, he talked for a long time about his depression this last month. He said he was feeling better, ready to resume his life. "A fog came over me. I can't explain it. It just came and filled my head. I felt so empty. So lacking in energy. Every morning I tried to get out of bed, but couldn't. I never felt so helpless. Even during the war when I was hospitalized for a month when a bomb blew me into a wall. That's when they shipped me back to the States before they transferred me to Europe. I couldn't move my arms for several days. But I felt more helpless in this fog. I'm better now. The fog has cleared."

I had never heard him—or any man— talk like this. Didn't know it was something men did. The men in the candy store talked about horses and football and baseball and money, but never uttered a word about their feelings, except anger at being screwed or gypped or unlucky. It was like the moment when I entered Yankee Stadium for the first time and came upon the light and the field—I felt a thrill. Maybe those weeks in bed had made him more sensitive, like my mother.

"How are you going to get the money for Nathan?"

"I've made some calls. I'm working on it."

"Do you think he'll come after you again?"

"Mind your own business. I'll handle Nathan. Now that I'm better, I can think clearly."

He stared at the round light fixture in the ceiling, and I had the feeling he was scheming ways of making money, things he wouldn't discuss with me. Not wanting to lose him, I asked about his time in China, the one topic he was always ready to talk about.

"The money was just coming at me. The Jews in China all trusted me. They had never seen a Jew like me. They were shopkeepers and businessmen. Very classy. They took me in like family. Treated me with respect. A Jewish warrior. They couldn't believe it. Their children idolized me and I let them punch me in the stomach as hard as they wanted. Ari followed me everywhere and today he's the most important lawyer in Israel. Invited your mother and me to stay with him, all expenses paid. Said we would be treated like royalty. These Jews were smart and rich and they would've done anything for me. Anything for Harry Davis."

His hands gestured in the air, recreating jeeps and rutted roads and conversations. He even revealed that he had been attracted to Chinese women, and his hands traced their figures. Then he turned to look at me and hesitated before saying, "Don't tell your mother, the sex in China was incredible."

"But you were already married."

"The rules are different during a war. We weren't really married yet. It was a war ceremony. We never lived together. I only got married because of the war. I never should have married your mother. I knew Rosie didn't think I was good enough for her. Always putting me down because I only went to eighth grade. If the Army had let me stay in China I would've come home a millionaire. Then what would Rosie have said? I was going away for at least two years. Your mother never liked my sisters because she was jealous of how close we all were. You see how controlling she is. Has to take over, has to be the star. Only because of the war I gave in and married her. She'd be single today if I hadn't given in."

"But she's so beautiful. Some other man would have married her."

"No one else would put up with her and her mother. You think another man is going to allow Rosie to live with him like I do? Look how nice it is without her here."

"I miss her," I said. I did. Her powdered smell, her warmth, her hand always touching me.

"I've got an ulcer because of her."

"Who else would you have married?"

"I don't know. Maybe I'd have been a bachelor. Lots of women, lots of sex, no commitments. I could have done things my way and been much more successful."

"But you love Mom, don't you?"

He made a face and shrugged and was silent for awhile. Neighbors across the courtyard were screaming at each other, something about buying the wrong cookies. Their voices grew tighter and louder. Then my father said, "I don't know what love is. Your mother and I are together. We have children. We do things for each other. We fight. We make up. She gets on my nerves. Would I sacrifice my life to protect her, sure. Do I appreciate her sometimes, sure. She makes me laugh. She's loyal. She's also not a faker. But what a pain in the ass."

"Sounds like love to me."

My father squeezed my thigh and laughed. If Mickey Mantle had hit a home run at Yankee Stadium and I had jumped up high in the bleachers and caught it with my glove it couldn't have felt any better than lying beside my father and hearing him talk openly for the first time.

With the Bar Mitzvah only a couple of days away, I played the Haftorah record at least thirty times each night before falling asleep, as well as practicing my speech for hours during the day. My mother was tense with Grandma in the hospital, screaming on the telephone, making final arrangements with the caterers. We hadn't invited Mara, or Tony, or the Spratz brothers. My parents didn't want Nathan to come, especially after what he he'd done to my father, but they were afraid of insulting him by asking him not to attend. Joe, from Joe's candy store, said he would come. Fat Bertha couldn't leave her post. My mother's boss, Arthur Posner, and his male companion, Norman, were invited but said they couldn't make it. My mother said that was probably for the best since other people weren't as open-minded as she was. Freddy, my favorite cousin, was also a homosexual, but he pretended that he wasn't, so he didn't upset anyone, though everyone knew the truth. He would come alone and dance with all the women and make them laugh and love him and join in the pretense. Since the Bar Mitzvah reception was in New Rochelle, only five of my friends were coming.

My mother had made a chart at work like a horse racing handicap sheet. She gave copies to Suzy and me. In the left column were all the invited guests. The next column was for our guesses as to how much money each guest would give me as a present. The third column was for the actual amount. The fourth was the difference plus or minus, and the right-hand column had my mother's handicap comments. For Aunt Sylvia she wrote, "Good in the mud. Erratic and cheap. Lucky if you get $10." For Cousin Harvey, the big doctor from her side of the family, she wrote, "Thoroughbred, good breeding, expect a payday. At least $100."

With my Haftorah playing in the background, I sat at my desk and filled out the chart. My mother said the winner, the one whose guesses were closest to the actual amounts, would get twenty dollars. Since it was probably the only Bar Mitzvah money I'd be allowed to keep, any cash gifts going directly to the caterer and Nathan, I took the contest seriously.

For my thirty-three year old cousin Sandra, who had a reputation for being promiscuous, my mother's comment was, "This filly likes a fast track. Will take on all stallions. Figure $40." For Cousin Freddy, she wrote, "Light on his feet, likes to come from behind. $50."

Playing this game was a welcome distraction from my losing struggle to memorize Hebrew and my sense of impending doom. My mother still assured me I would be a hit. In fact, everyone including Rabbi Skulnick said I would do fine. I was the only one who knew how unprepared I was to be a man.

# 20.

I stood sweating in my powder blue tuxedo beside the rabbi. His head came up to my shoulders. With the sun streaming through the stained glass windows it must've been 110 degrees inside the un-air-conditioned synagogue. Some men had already taken off their suit jackets, loosened their ties, and opened the top buttons on their shirts. Women fanned themselves with their hands and Bar Mitzvah programs. I still couldn't remember more than a couple of Hebrew words but Rabbi Skulnick had kindly translated my Haftorah into English and then slipped me the cheat sheet right before the ceremony. The problem was that I couldn't read his handwriting.

I stared out at the congregation: my mother in her orange dress and my father with the white tallis draped over his shoulders, my parents' friends, my father's crazy sisters, my friends, Cousin Joel and fat Cousin Harvey, also known as Dr. Mandlestein, who my mother was always bragging about, thin and handsome Cousin Freddy, and Nathan, wearing a silver yarmulke on his greasy hair. Grandma was still in the hospital so neither she nor Mr. Fein came.

"Today, Ricky becomes a man," Rabbi Skulnick said for the third time. His voice was gravelly, like he had stones in his mouth. I was happy for him to drone on. Maybe we'd run out of time and just skip my part altogether.

"It's not easy to become a man. Not easy to be a man in the modern world with so many distractions and temptations. Punchball, stickball, handball: Ricky would have liked to play those games after school. Instead he chose a tradition with much meaning for him, and for us."

My father's sisters and their husbands sat in the back of the sanctuary where the sunlight, filtering through the two large stained glass windows, lit up the last few rows with a rainbow of color. Aunt Ruthie, in a long green dress that she had shoplifted from Macy's, fanned herself with the program. Aunt Sylvia, wearing violet looked as if vomit was already stirring in her gut. She lifted her skirt above her knees, spread her legs, opened a prayer book, and used it as a fan. I glanced down at the cheat sheet and beads of sweat dripped off my face.

"Ricky Davis is a fine example of Jewish youth. He has worked hard and proven to me that he deserves to be called the second highest title a boy can achieve...a man. And I know in time he will earn the highest title: a good man, a mensch." He patted me on the shoulder and walked to the other side of the bimah.

Unable to speak, I stood there, looking out at my friends and family, and at the congregants who weren't invited to my Bar Mitzvah but attended synagogue every Saturday morning, mostly old men and women. The audience started to grow restless. I could hear grumbling, and my friends giggling. I squinted, trying to decipher the rabbi's handwriting.

"Barru ah mel mel mel," I said. I stuttered a few more Hebrew syllables before falling silent. My mind totally blanked out. Even the few Hebrew words I had memorized vanished. My hands felt clammy and the cheat sheet slipped to the floor. Strange sounds started coming out of my throat, sounds that had no connection to Hebrew—or English. The closest resemblance to any sounds that I had ever heard was the braying of a donkey.

"Vut is going on here?" one of the old congregants shouted.

"Is there something wrong with him?" an old woman asked.

Like someone speaking in tongues, I heehawed for what felt like over a minute. (I was later told the braying lasted only about twenty seconds.) With the congregants shouting, and my aunts and uncles talking among themselves, my friends laughing, and others shushing the talkers, the hubbub competed with my bizarre sounds.

Luckily, Rabbi Skulnick was not a stickler for orthodoxy. He moved into emergency mode and stuck his hand behind the curtain, adjusting the arm of the record player, which he'd already cued up with his copy of the record we'd made at Woolworth's.

As the audience quieted, I starting mouthing the Hebrew chants on the record. I must've looked like an out-of-sync singer on television because my friends became hysterical, laughing and slapping each other. Cousin Joel's loud whinny sounded like a dentist's drill, and knowing that he was taking pleasure in my suffering caused me to compulsively run my hands along my thighs and blink my eyes.

I tried to ignore the commotion as I mouthed the Hebrew words. My father had his head down but my mother smiled at me. Though Suzy, nine months pregnant, was taking deep breaths as the sweat poured down her face, she too smiled encouragingly.

Until that morning as I stood in front of the congregation, the poor sound quality on the two- dollar record hadn't seemed that important, and the background noise of the lunch counter and the female voice had been irrelevant. But in the splendid acoustics of the synagogue, the voice sounded loud and clear. And it wasn't the voice of God. It was the waitress at Woolworth's shouting her order to the short-order cook in a piercing Bronx accent. "Two eggs sunny side up. Hash browns on the side. Four eggs scrambled. Extra bacon."

I kept moving my lips, but I was fully conscious that I had already blown my Bar Mitzvah. I had totally undermined whatever meaning was in the ritual, the thousands of years of boys becoming men.

The record was almost done when the needle got stuck on a scratch and it started repeating. I mouthed the same Hebrew words over and over. I improvised a cough to cover the scratch. Rabbi Skulnick allowed the record to repeat nine times before he snuck his hand behind the curtain and gave the needle a shove.

When it was over there was no standing ovation like in my fantasies, but at least I wasn't making animal sounds anymore. My mother nodded that it was okay. Her cousin Eva tossed me kisses, and Cousin Freddy gave me two thumbs up. Suzy, rubbing her belly with both hands, gave me with the warmest smile I had ever seen. It seemed to convey that we had endured all of Grandma's burnt pot roasts and all of our parents' fights and screaming, and we could endure this as well. For a second,

I thought, paraphrasing my grandmother, "I can answer the phone. I'm a person."

"No you can't," my father seemed to say by saying nothing, by looking at the floor as if he was too ashamed to look at his son.


The ballroom at the Riviera Beach Club overlooked Long Island Sound. The grounds were lit, showcasing the pool and cabanas and the beach. In the middle of the ballroom a large chandelier hung high above the round tables that were set for eight with embroidered table cloths and floral-patterned china and centerpieces of red, yellow, and white freesias. The guests mingled outside the ballroom in the foyer where the smorgasbord was taking place. Hot meatballs, Jell-O molds, slaws, shish kebob, caviar, chopped liver, melon balls, and chicken thighs and breasts were spread out on long tables. Waitresses carrying trays of cocktail franks weaved through the guests. Once the guests were stuffed the doors to the ballroom opened and the guests sat down to eat giant prime ribs and fruit cocktails and drink champagne and gorge on éclairs, chocolate pies and canned whipped cream. And then dance off the extra pounds to the music of Max Katz and his eight-piece Kool Katz Klub.

My mother looked exceptionally beautiful in her orange dress mamboing with my father in his white tuxedo. She raised the long gown, exposing her ankles and calves. There was something magic in the air, which was fragrant from the freesias. My parents lit up the dance floor. Other dancing couples stopped to watch. For the moment Pearl didn't look like a middle-aged secretary but more like a young singer spinning in Harry's arms, winning all the dance contests, the envy of all the girls. They were that couple, from her stories of the Catskills, whose dreams still had velocity.

I danced with Suzy who was a week overdue. She waddled more than danced in her pink maternity dress. When the band changed beats to a foxtrot, my father and I switched partners.

"Mom told me you still don't have enough money to pay off Nathan or the Bar Mitzvah," Suzy said loud enough for my mother and me to hear. "I spoke to Jeffrey again, but he won't lend you any money. Not even to pay the band."

My father shot my mother an angry look when he heard this. "Don't worry about it," he said tensely. "With Ricky's gifts we can pay the remaining Bar Mitzvah bills."

"What about Nathan?"

"I don't need help from my pregnant daughter."

"I feel bad; you always gave to me."

"Forget it," he said abruptly. He looked over again at my mother. She and I danced across the room, away from him and Suzy.

When the music stopped, Suzy went back to her table. My father strode toward us with an incensed look in his eyes. Rather than retreat my mother held her ground. I sensed a scene in the making. "Mom, please," I said.

Luckily, Nathan cut in to claim his promised dance. Max Katz and the Kool Katz Klub began an imitation of Elvis Presley singing "Hound Dog." Nathan grabbed my mother's hand and twirled her around in a wild Lindy. He didn't dance as gracefully as my father, but he was on beat, kicking his feet between her legs, and bumping into her body. He spun her and caught her, cradling her with both arms, her back pressed against his chest.

My father didn't look happy. Aunt Ruthie asked him to dance

and whisked him away. He didn't see Nathan whisper something into my mother's ear that made her wince. His view was blocked by other dancers so he didn't notice Nathan's hands touch her arm, her shoulder, her back, and brush her breasts as she spun. Had it been another man, I probably wouldn't have noticed either. Touching was part of dancing close. But this was Nathan. I'd already witnessed his slug-like tongue slip out of her mouth after he'd made her sing to him that morning in our apartment.

He put his hand on her hip and pulled her close. His lips touched her ear and she snapped her head back.

I decided to cut in before my father saw what was going on. Nathan, no longer on beat, now held her from behind and pressed against her ass. His pelvis rocked forward. My mother jerked and tried to push him away, but he held her tightly and rubbed against her. It all happened so quickly, on a crowded dance floor, the music loud, the dancers wild, that no one seemed to notice except for my mother and me.

"My turn," I said, grabbing my mother's arm and pulling her away.

"Oh, there's the Bar Mitzvah boy," Nathan said. He reached into his pocket and handed me an envelope. "I've had a wonderful time but I have to be going."

My mother looked angry when he leaned closer to whisper something. She moved away, not allowing him to touch her. As she did, his voice grew louder. "...I need you."

The music stopped and he tried to kiss her goodbye, but she dodged her face to the left, then to the right, so his lips only made air kisses. "Your mother won't even give me a goodbye kiss," he said to me. "Maybe I should steal a kiss from your sister."

My mother froze, then smiled, and kissed him on

the cheek.

"You can do better than that," he said. He pointed to his lips.

She gave me a pained glance, and then lifted her face to him. He sneered and moved as if to kiss her but instead he said, "Yom Kippur" and he walked away.

My mother and Nathan were not the only ones who danced close and rubbed against each other that night. Cousin Sandra and I danced slowly to "Chances Are." She was heavily perfumed and I breathed her in as my cheek rested against hers. At first I held her with my right arm around her back and my left hand near her shoulder, the way my sister had taught me to foxtrot. But Cousin Sandra threw her arms around me and pressed tightly against my body. I couldn't have fitted any more snugly against her unless we were attached. She had to feel my erection but she said nothing about it and neither did I. We just danced and she sang softly into my ear, *Well, chances are you're chances are awfully good.*

When the song was over she didn't let go until almost all the dancers were off the floor. As she did, her hand slid across my crotch. It could have been accidental, but the way she smiled and said, "Love dancing with you," I didn't think so. It was a Bar Mitzvah gift. One that my mother hadn't handicapped, but that I always treasured.

"I told you not to ask Susan for money," my father said to my mother as we sat at the dais, a long rectangular table set on a platform facing the ballroom and the view of Long Island Sound. An almost full moon lit the water. Two sailboats rocked in the distance.

"Not now, Harry. Let's just enjoy the Bar Mitzvah."

"You always have to butt in."

"Jeffrey is showing you up," I said, nodding at the dance floor. It was no longer a question of if they were going to have a fight, but simply when. I hoped it could be put off until the guests went home. I squeezed my mother's arm.

"Ricky's right. People are saying Jeffrey is a better cha cha dancer than you."

"I'm tired." My father looked weary, his tuxedo jacket and tie gone, his shirt unbuttoned to the middle of his chest.

"I guess we'll just have to settle for second place," my mother said.

He smiled a smile that said he knew he was being baited, diverted from his anger, but it could wait. We all knew that he was too competitive to resist a challenge. He rose from his chair as if the sixty remaining guests had come solely to see him perform his magic. In a second he was leaping gracefully off the platform and spinning my mother as he pivoted and twirled and paused and shook his hips. It was quite a cha cha. Equal to the great cha cha they had danced at Cousin Joel's Bar Mitzvah. Their bodies, though tired and signaling mutual resentment, still could work harmoniously together on the dance floor. Her curvy shape was perfect for the cha cha, each movement of her hips and shoulders clearly articulated in the rocking back and forth and side to side. He took her hand and lead her into a chasse to the left, cha cha cha, and then to the right, cha cha cha.

Most of the guests formed a circle around them and Jeffrey

who was dancing with Cousin Sandra. On the sideline Suzy waved her arms, trying to get his attention.

The spectators oohed and ahhed and applauded for more. My father requested "In the Mood" for an encore. Jeffrey and Cousin Sandra joined Suzy on the sidelines as my parents carved up the dance floor, swinging each other in perfectly choreographed arcs and kicks and cuddles. They were magical. They seemed so happy, so in sync with each other. And they weren't just putting on a show, that was the amazing thing. For those moments on the dance floor, their joy was real, their anger forgotten, as their bodies moved to the beat of the other. Or so it seemed to me.

Right before the music stopped, my father made his signature jive move, leaping high in the air, throwing his legs to the side, and touching his toes. It was after eleven. Nathan, Cousin Freddy, Aunt Sylvia, and my friends were already gone. My father, winded, grasped my mother roughly by the arm as she walked off the dance floor. He said loudly, "I don't need help from my pregnant daughter."

"Again with that?"

"Next time I tell you not to ask her for money, don't go behind my back."

"Where are you going to get the money?"

"I'll get it. I have ideas."

"What kind of ideas? Giving borrowed money to Holocaust survivors?"

"Shut up!" he screamed.

"Shut up yourself, you loser! Tax-free cigarettes! Fireproof pajamas! You got ideas?"

"Shut up!"

A hundred eyes stared at them. My father wiped his face with the back of his hand. My mother watched him deflate on the edge of the dance floor. She looked like she was weighing her options. She could grab him now, and nudge him onto the dance floor, and lead him into a Peabody or jitterbug or foxtrot, and all would be temporarily forgotten. The guests would resume dancing and eating more dessert and laughing. But as it happened, the Kool Katz Klub was taking a short break, and she chose to fight.

"Shut up yourself, you Bronx *cutter*. My mother has to have more liver tests next week. Any extra money will be eaten up by doctor bills."

"No more doctors!" My father exploded. Blood rushed to his neck and face.

"No more doctors. No more doctors. You dumb *cutter*. You cheap stupid *cutter!*" She attacked him with her fists.

He put up his arms to block her punches, but he didn't fight back.

"Pearl, come on, it's a Bar Mitzvah," Cousin Eva shouted.

My mother shot her such a look of contempt that Cousin Eva backed off. Raging, my mother stepped away, her fists futile against him, trying to hurt him with words instead. "Moron! Shmuck!" She fumbled through her vocabulary. "Loser! *Cutter!*"

I sat watching from the dais. Suzy, walked over to me with tears in her eyes. I offered her a chocolate chip cookie. "Come sit down, enjoy the fight. This is the best seat in the house."

"How can you just sit there and watch?"

"Those Davises really know how to throw an affair." We both knew that humor was the safe route we always took in times like this, but she didn't laugh. She started sobbing.

"It's the baby," she said, forcing a smile. "Hormones."

We both looked down at our mother, who was still ranting. Hate transformed her face. Her high cheekbones and sharp angles had tightened into a witch's profile. This fight had been brewing for hours, maybe months. Years. Who knew what it was really about? "Kike," she bellowed.

Some of the guests groaned. Our father stood there, his hands hanging down, his head bowed, accepting the public whipping. She circled him, crouching lower. Searching, it seemed, for some word that would destroy him. Like a haircut for Samson or a piece of kryptonite for Superman.

"You you you *Doctor Hater!*" The words hung in the air, freezing the guests, stopping time—*Doctor Hater!*

Then, as passionately as she had screamed, my mother began to laugh, wild belly laughter, as the absurdity of the insult took purchase. She tried to repeat "Doctor Hater," but each time she formed the words, laughter came out instead. She dropped to the ground and hugged my father's legs, vibrating against him.

He fell to his knees, shaking with laughter. The two of them laughed uncontrollably against each other. I laughed. Suzy burst out laughing, holding her belly, as if the baby too was laughing, wanting to get out of the womb and be part of the family fun.

Suddenly Suzy started moaning. At first I thought the baby might've kicked her too hard. Then I saw the puddle on the floor. She began sweating profusely and taking deep breaths.

Meanwhile my mother pulled herself onto her knees. Parodying herself she held onto my father and tried to glare and mutter, "you you doctor ha—," but they both tumbled over laughing onto the dance floor.

"I'm going to have a baby," Suzy shouted. Our parents rose to their feet and rushed over. Cousin Harvey, the doctor, volunteered to drive with Suzy and Jeffrey to the hospital. My parents and I followed right behind in my father's rusted out Ford convertible.

In the waiting room, my mother and I passed the time, adding up the cash gifts and comparing them to our guesses and her handicap comments.

"You're really good at this," she said, marveling at how close my guesses were to the actual amounts given.

"Maybe I could become a professional gift handicapper." She laughed, but when she looked over at my father sleeping in a plastic chair, she quickly changed the subject. Maybe my skill reminded her too much of his handicapping ability when he was younger or maybe it was knowing that even with the Bar Mitvzah money they were still in trouble. When added to loans from friends, they were still $19,000 short of what they owed Nathan.

When a nurse came in to tell us that Suzy had a healthy baby girl, my mother clapped her hands and cried, "This is a blessing from God." Nine hours after we'd arrived at the hospital, the cry of seven-pound-two-ounce Marjorie, my parent's first grandchild, brought immense joy to the best family in the Bronx. For the Bar Mitzvah boy, dancing close with Cousin Sandra, winning twenty dollars in the gift competition, and becoming an uncle, turned out to be a wonderful introduction to manhood.

# 21.

Three days before Yom Kippur, my mother sat eating Mallomars at our kitchen table. She was telling me about her moral dilemma that afternoon at her office. As she talked she looked around at the black wall telephone, the clock with the menorah sitting on top of it, the window facing the courtyard, and the raggedy potholders hanging on a nail. With Bar Mitzvah gifts and hocked wedding rings and small loans from friends she and my father had managed to pay off almost a third of what they owed Nathan. But with a 40 percent a month interest rate on most of the borrowed money, they still owed him almost twenty thousand dollars. As far as she was concerned she had only two viable choices. Either she could ask her boss if she could borrow money from the firm, which would be deducted from her wages each week or she could take money out of Elizabeth Taylor's account. Both plans had their shortcomings. Arthur Posner was a wonderful man but he was cheap, and she knew he might turn her down. If he did, she would loathe him, which wouldn't be good for her job. Also, he was helping her negotiate with the supermarket's insurance company. A settlement was still months if not years away and she knew she would get more money if he stayed involved.

Though she had no qualms about certain illegal activities like shoplifting, stealing from Elizabeth Taylor or "borrowing for awhile" as she called it, wasn't an act she took lightly. Arthur trusted her. Clients like Orson Welles and Otto Preminger and Rock Hudson and Vivian Leigh trusted her and had become friends with her. She had total access to the accounts the firm managed. Many of their celebrity clients were not particularly good with money. The system of Arthur supervising their bank accounts and investments worked well only as long as everyone with access was honest. Arthur was impeccably ethical and at work my mother had been the same. The clients knew that their money was safe in her hands. She had always bragged about that to me.

The mechanics of sneaking $20,000 from Elizabeth Taylor's account seemed relatively simple since millions flowed in and out each year and Elizabeth didn't pay much attention and her husband, Eddie Fisher, didn't have access to the account. Besides, my mother was positive that she would be able to put money back before tax season when the accountants would be looking over things more carefully.

Still, even as she told me an edited version of events, stuffing herself with cookies, I had the feeling she was trying to convince me, and maybe herself, that what she'd done that afternoon was somehow acceptable.

She said that the work day had begun normally enough, although when she was taking dictation, Arthur had asked if everything was alright, so she must have been showing anxiety.

"Fine," she said.

"Kids are okay?"

"Fine…I just get edgy in the summer."

"I know." His mustache crowded his nose when he smiled, rising up on the ends. His office walls were filled with pictures of him smiling alongside Lauren Bacall and Anthony Quinn and Charlton Heston and Zero Mostel and Angela Lansbury and hundreds of other stars.

"I want you to call David Merrick. Put me through when you get a hold of him."

She left his office. A couple of times during the afternoon she placed her hand on her phone to call the bank but she kept putting it off, typing letters. The banks would be closing in two hours and she didn't want to have to go through another day like this. When Elizabeth Taylor called, it spooked her. She only wanted to know about some house seats to see Dick Van Dyke in *Bye Bye Birdie*. But she was so friendly.

After that call my mother lost her nerve. What if her boss found out? He would just sit there in his leather chair, shaking his head, maybe saying, "Pearl, how could you do that?" genuinely hurt. How could he comprehend, having been raised by a wealthy family to be a lawyer? Private schools in New England, Harvard, Yale Law, and a life full of celebrities and parties and acclaim. He had never experienced a moment when he couldn't pay an electric bill or buy a coat or go out to dinner. He had no clue what it meant to have a gangster like Nathan Glucksman hounding him.

She resigned herself to asking him for the loan, so she went back to his office and closed the door, feeling relief that she'd come to her senses. He was on the phone and signaled her to sit down. He was joking with Mike Nichols, whose comedy show, *An evening with Mike Nichols and Elaine May*, was due to open on Broadway in a month.

When he hung up he was still laughing. He leaned back in his chair. "What can I do for you, Pearl?"

She burst out crying and proceeded to tell him about Nathan and the money that was due. Immediately she saw that it was a mistake. The way his smile vanished, his jaw turned hard, and his body stiffened. His bushy mustache frowned over his lips.

"Pearl, you're the best secretary I ever had. I would do anything to keep you, but you can't come into my office, start weeping, and expect me to give you twenty thousand dollars because your husband has gambling debts. That's so unfair of you. It puts me in a terrible position. We don't know if and when the supermarket will settle. I could be taking money out of your weekly salary for years. It's too messy. You know I don't like messes. I'm sorry, but it simply is out of the question."

"I have nowhere else to turn."

"I'm sure you and this Nathan can work it out. You said he's an old friend of yours."

"He's a monster."

"This is very upsetting to me. I have to deal with so many crises in our clients' lives. You know better than anyone how much attention Carol and Orson and Otto need. I can't take on the personal problems of my employees as well. I don't have the time or energy. Please, I don't want to talk about it anymore."

My mother went back to her desk and cried for fifteen minutes. As she'd anticipated, she began to loathe him. He had the money. The business had the money. After all she had done for him. It was just so selfish. The way he just looked away from her, dismissing her.

As her thoughts turned bitter it became easier to make the bank transfer. She no longer cared about his horror if he found out she had borrowed money from Elizabeth Taylor. She could atone for the temporary theft at synagogue in a few days. It's not like she planned to keep the money. It was only a loan. She'd be happy to pay interest. She could deposit some extra money or she could send Elizabeth some cash anonymously, a present for the loan. Elizabeth didn't need the extra money—she didn't even need the twenty thousand dollars—but Pearl would pay it back plus extra because it was the right thing to do. Besides, once there was a settlement with the supermarket she could return all the money immediately, no harm done.

Her mood began to change. She started to feel good about herself, that she was clever enough to plan the bank transfer and cover her tracks, and noble enough to return all the money with interest. Only an extraordinary person would do that.

"Elizabeth Taylor should send me a thank-you note," she joked to me before continuing her story.

She had a lovely conversation with Anthony Newly, one of her favorite clients. She typed up two letters. Then she told the receptionist she was going out on an errand and would be back in ten minutes.

She walked along Fifth Avenue in her high heels. The sun felt marvelous on her face. She should do this more often, she thought, get out for a walk during work. If she counted all the lunch breaks she had worked through, all the times she had stayed late to finish a letter, a contract, all without any extra compensation, she was owed much more than she had asked him to borrow. He should be giving her the money as a bonus.

With interest. She had earned it.

She hummed "Save the Last Dance for Me" as she strolled by Saks and looked in the windows at the fall dresses and sweaters. She stopped at the drugstore and picked up some shampoo and Lucky Strikes. Then she crossed the street, and pulled hard on the tall glass doors of the bank, went inside and embezzled twenty-thousand dollars.

As she finished her story, she lit her first cigarette in over a year. "I don't think I'll get caught."

"Mom, you should return it tomorrow."

"The bank is closed on Saturdays."

"Then on Monday."

"It's Yom Kippur."

"You don't want to go to jail. They don't serve Mallomars there. No seven-layer cake. No éclairs."

"Good. I could lose a little weight." She shoved a whole Mallomar into her mouth.

"No Broadway shows. No dancing. No grandchildren. Marilyn Monroe won't be visiting you. Certainly not Elizabeth Taylor."

"I have no choice. I'm not going to let a fucking monster like Nathan harm my husband or lay a hand on me."

"But..."

"I'm just borrowing it for awhile." She told me that even if she got caught, she knew that neither her boss nor Elizabeth Taylor would want to press charges so it was unlikely she would end up in jail, though she would lose her job.

"How long before the accountants figure out the money is missing?" I asked. She blew smoke at me. Through the haze my mother's face looked distant and wistful.

# 22.

The day of atonement arrived. As a family we needed it. For me dropping the egg had been my biggest sin of the year. Grandma was still in the hospital. The last time I visited her she'd been sleeping with tubes down her nose, her mouth wide open, and her false teeth resting on a dish on the bedside table. She looked like she was already dead. Breaking her pelvis was not life threatening in itself, but all of her systems seemed to fail after that. Her kidneys, her liver, her bowels, shutting down as if her pelvis was her body's main conductor of electricity and the break had blown her circuits. Her blood pressure rose into the danger zone. Her heart beat irregularly.

As I sat watching her chest rise and fall, my eyes occasionally darted to her teeth, which seemed to be watching me. Perhaps because they had starred in so many important roles in my pillow fights, those teeth felt very much alive, waiting for a chance to get back into the action.

Grandma was on my mind as I walked to the synagogue

with my parents, all dressed up. I felt guilty for having helped her with the scam and for not revealing my crime to my mother. My parents were silent and I wondered if it was just the seriousness of the holiday or if they too felt guilty about their sins and having to confess to God. Though they must've been relieved that they now had the money to pay off Nathan, they seemed depressed. It was obvious that my mother, despite her rationalizations, felt bad that she had betrayed her boss's trust. My father was harder to read but I assumed he felt ashamed of being unable to pay Nathan back without his wife's help, not to mention the shame of hanging helpless from a fish hook.

When we arrived, the synagogue was packed with men in suits, tallises and yarmulkes and women dressed in their finest clothes. Almost all of the seats were taken. People stood in the side aisles and in the back. Although it was an Indian summer day, already in the eighties, several women sported fur jackets. My mother wore a pale blue dress, my father a black suit, and I had on my brown sport jacket and a red tie.

I thought about Grandma. With each mournful prayer and each chant and song my eyes welled with tears. At one point I was filled with so much sadness that I had to sit down, though it was a prayer where the congregation was supposed to remain standing. My father kept looking over and raising his hand for me to rise.

"Leave him alone," my mother whispered.

When the mourners sang the Kaddish, the prayer for the dead, I wept. I knew that next year I would be singing along with them, chanting and swaying and remembering my grandmother, a life coming to an end—eighty-four years. Not in this synagogue, but another because we were moving to New

Rochelle in four weeks. My mother certain that eventually the supermarket would give us a big settlement took a free limousine ride to New Rochelle over the weekend and found an apartment in one day. Then she came home and announced that we were moving. She told us she no longer could live in the Bronx.

Rabbi Skulnick, looking dapper in his silver tallis and silver yarmulke, stood on the bimah facing the congregation to give his Yom Kippur Sermon. With the opened torah unveiled behind him, the scroll of Hebrew letters forming a lovely abstract graphic, he spoke about breaking commandments, about selfishness and not reaching out and helping others. I thought about my sins. I had a lot to atone for. He instructed us not to be mean, not to hate, not to embarrass, not to insult or harm with words, and not to avenge or even bear a grudge. "This is what the Talmud teaches us." He paused, clearing his throat and wiping his forehead. "This is Halakah. This is the path we must take as Jews."

I shook my head, listening hard. I acknowledged most of these sins and vowed to be better, but I couldn't see how I could let go of my desire for revenge against Tony or my grudge against Nathan. I would be better, but not perfect.

When Rabbi Skulnick said to take a moment of silence to think about the loved ones we'd lost, I cheated and thought of Grandma even though she was still alive. She had sacrificed herself to try to help our family. I thought about the sacrifices my mother was willing to make to help her husband. I turned my head to my father, who had thrown himself on a bomb to save his Army buddies, and I knew that he would sacrifice himself to save his wife or daughter or son. This was my family; they had their flaws, but it was nice to know they were on my side.

I said a silent prayer. "*Grandma please get well. Please God don't punish her for my sins. I'll be better. I love her. Her touch. Her smell. Her ancient ways. I love her and want her back in our house. I won't lose patience with her. I won't be sneaky anymore. I won't hump my pillows. I won't lie or cheat or speak ill of anyone. Just make her well.*"

Rabbi Skulnick said, "Take another moment of silence and think about yourself. How you could be better and help others more and be more loving and more compassionate."

I thought about all the cowardly and selfish things I had done in the last few months: stealing my father's money, touching Mara's private parts, badgering her to strip for my friends, coming to her rescue too late, licking Tony and wanting him dead, fantasizing killing Nathan, dropping the egg. I wondered if I'd exceeded the limit for Yom Kippur forgiveness and would be disqualified for atonement. If God did exist, then it was nice of him to provide a Yom Kippur, like a laundromat for the soul.

As I walked home after the services I felt shaky, weak from fasting. My parents stayed at the synagogue to talk to friends. Other Jews observing the holiday filled the sidewalks and I walked part of the way with two older boys who lived around the corner from me. They invited me to play poker.

"On Yom Kippur?"

"Why not?"

"I don't know; it doesn't seem right."

"We're playing at Larry's house at two. It'll be fun."

"Maybe."

There was no way I was going back around the block to

play cards. I wanted only to drink some water and lay on the couch. But when I reached my building I felt too weak to even climb the courtyard stoop. I staggered down the alley ramp to the basement to take the elevator.

As I approached the door I thought I heard Mara. I walked around the building and thirty feet away I saw Tony pinning her on the ground against the trash cans. He wore his trademark sweaty white t-shirt. He wedged his knee between her thighs and slipped his monstrous hand inside her blouse.

He was grinning, a toothpick in his mouth, and Mara was squirming, trying to get free. Neither of them had seen me yet, so I had time to sneak away. The excuses for fleeing flooded my brain. I was so weak from fasting, what could I do? If I ran, I could get help. I could call the police. I was moving out of the Bronx soon; this wasn't my problem. Mara wasn't my friend anymore. My legs felt rubbery. Tony was massive.

The image of my grandmother marching across the supermarket floor, bread in hand, appeared like a ghost. I tried to summon her courage.

"Leave her alone," I shouted, running toward them.

Tony swiveled his head. Mara whimpered, looking frightened. He tore open her blouse, his hand pulling at her bra.

I stood over him. "Get off her, Tony."

With one hand on her breast, he grabbed my ankle with his free hand and yanked me to the ground. I started to get up. He pinned Mara with his knee, let go of her breast, and used both of his hands to pull me, by my sport jacket, toward them. Mara, kicking, picked up a metal trash can cover and hit him on the head.

Mara was almost to her feet when he knocked her back

down. I threw myself at him. With my skinny arm around his neck I pulled him backward, giving her enough time to stand up.

She raised the trashcan cover to hit him again. "Run Mara, don't worry about me. Run. Run."

He threw me off easily and blocked her blow, sending the lid clanging against the cans. He grabbed her wrist. I wrapped my arm around his thick sweaty neck again, trying to strangle him. His foul odor made me feel like I was going to faint. Mara bit hard on his hand and he let go with a howl. This time she ran.

Enraged, Tony stood up, shaking his hand. He broke my stranglehold, twisted my arm behind my back and lifted me up over his head before hurling me into the trashcans. Three of the cans toppled over. I lay on the concrete, bleeding, and covered in trash as Tony stood over me with a rabid look in his eyes.

"So you've come back for more," he said, grabbing his crotch. "You like the taste of dick."

I shook my head and tried to back up, knocking against a trash can.

"Where you going all dressed up?"

"It's Yom Kippur. A Jewish holiday."

He grinned. He grabbed my tie and started choking me. "How much money you got...Jew? You must've gotten a lot of money at your Bar Mitzvah. Why didn't you invite me?"

"Let me go, Tony."

I reached for two quarters that were in my sport jacket. Jews weren't supposed to carry money on Yom Kippur anyway. I rose to my knees and handed over the quarters but he still yanked on my tie.

"I want this tie." He yanked harder, hoisted me up and then

dragged me across the alley, banging into trashcans, tearing my pants, scraping skin off my knees.

I was dizzy and humiliated. I wanted to stop him, but I couldn't.

"Give it to me," he said, letting go.

I struggled to untie the knot, but his yanking had tightened it. "Give it to me you little kike."

"Don't call me that," I said, still trying to loosen the knot.

He grabbed me by my hair and pulled me up. "What did you say, kike?" He shoved me back on the ground. I looked up at his broad copper chest and black hairy underarms and short, thick neck. It was a strange body on a strange boy, stumpy arms and legs, like a mutant, like maybe God had made a mistake.

"Don't call me that." The words came out of my mouth on their own.

He kicked me in the ribs. "Kike."

"Don't call me that."

He kicked me harder. "Kike."

"Don't call me that."

He kicked me in the face. My nose started gushing blood.

"Kike."

"Don't call me that."

I let the blood flow across my lips and drop off my chin. This was a dumb game I was playing, a game Tony seemed far better at, but I felt myself grow stronger. I could feel my will rooting to the concrete and sense my grandmother on the supermarket linoleum and my parents sprawled on the Riviera dance floor.

"Kike."

"Don't call me that."

He kicked me in the ribs and abdomen. I moaned, gasping for air. He lifted his foot to kick me again but hesitated.

A window opened. Maybe a neighbor had heard all the noise? The window shut.

"Kike."

"Don't say that, Tony," I said, in as firm a voice as I could.

"Stop being nutty," he shouted. "Kike."

The next kick came to my heart but it didn't have the full force of his weight behind it. As if I was training a dog, I commanded, "Don't call me that!"

A strange look came over his face. His eyes wouldn't stay focused. His usually solid fist was shaking a little. "What the hell happened to you? It's the Bar Mitzvah isn't it? Some Jew voodoo?"

He backed away, as if he sensed my new strength. He opened the fist that clenched the two quarters, and looked at his hand as if they were burning a hole through his palm. He threw the quarters at me and backed further away.

"Stay away from me," he barked, backpedaling. "I'm warning you, stay away from me or I'll kill you."

He disappeared around the building. I heard him thumping up the alley as I lay on the ground, my nose hemorrhaging. The sky was a perfect cobalt blue, not a cloud visible. I breathed in the beautiful hot day through my mouth.

I held my white yarmulke against my nose like a compress and tried to find the strength to rise. The blood soaked into the fabric. It filled my mouth. I felt like I was bleeding from inside my gut.

I started laughing and blood streamed out of my mouth. New blood flowed in. I let some accumulate on my tongue and then I spit it straight up like a red geyser rising toward the blue sky. It separated into droplets and splattered across my face. I tasted my blood, and it tasted good.

Mara came running toward me with a towel in each hand and knelt beside me. I patted her knee. She smiled at me as if all the sins of the past were forgiven. She held a corner of the dry towel against my nose to slow the bleeding. With the wet towel she washed away my blood.

It felt so soothing. I wanted her to continue stroking. She must have sensed that because she kept nursing my wounds and dabbing my face long after the bleeding had stopped.

Then she kissed me on my lips. Something she had never done before, a real kiss. It hurt where Tony had kicked my upper lip, but I didn't care. I kissed her back. She cradled my head in her hands, lifting my face up to hers, and she kissed me again.

I wondered if Rabbi Skulnick would approve of making out with a shiksa in a trashcan alley on Yom Kippur, the holiest day of the year. Maybe I should be upstairs in my apartment, thinking about my life, how I could be a better human being in the eyes of God. Maybe I should be sitting beside my grandmother's hospital bed, nursing her back to health the way she had always nursed me. But the kissing was divine, and in terms of atonement I felt I was heeding God's commandment.

# 23.

My father waited till after sundown, when Yom Kippur was officially over to drive to Nathan's apartment in Riverdale. My mother refused to go along so I volunteered. When we arrived on the eighth-floor, we found that Nathan was hosting a break fast party.

A maid answered the door and invited us in but my father said we would wait in the hall. Twenty minutes later she came back and told us that Nathan was busy but he insisted we come in and eat. When my father said again that he preferred to wait in the hall, she said that Nathan had instructed her that when "'Harry says no, you tell him not to insult me.'"

After a moment we walked in. The apartment was huge, filled with so many wall-to-wall mirrors and chandeliers and ornate gold-leaf clocks that I got dizzy as I walked from room to room. While my father talked to some men that he knew, I hung out near the buffet table, which was spread with slices of roast beef and salami and tongue and pumpernickel and rye and potato salad and coleslaw and kosher pickles and lox and bagels.

Except for the maid, there were no women present. Most of the men looked like underworld figures, and the others I assumed were storekeepers and small businessmen who used Nathan as a Shylock.

My Bar Mitzvah had given me a license to join the Men's Club, but I felt like it could be revoked at any minute. I needed a guide into this manhood thing. I was barely thirteen, and I had a sense of what was right, and a hunch of what it meant to be a man, a human, a mensch, a good person. The opposite of Nathan, that unmensch, smiling like a phony—a real faker—making the rounds at his party.

"Faker," I whispered under my breath. Ditto for the businessmen laughing loudly at Nathan's stupid jokes. They made me angry. I might be sneaky and cowardly, but so what. I wasn't a faker; I was a good boy, a good man.

I saw no role models among these men. My father, the obvious choice seemed too flawed and too preoccupied with his own demons to lead the way. He stood next to a display of glass figurines. I studied him from different perspectives in the mirrors—right profile, left, head on. His hazel eyes, at times, glanced back at me, but his mind seemed to be somewhere else. Who was this man? A cutter, a bookie, a guy who had dropped out of school after eighth grade to help support his mother and crazy sisters, a boy, who according to legend, the other boys had worshipped, a war hero who came back from World War II with forty thousand dollars in illicit gains, a debt collector who gave Morris the money to go to Israel, an athlete who could throw a ball farther, hit a ball harder, and dance a cha cha that could take your breath away. Who was this man, my father? Even with our talk during the summer—sex is everything, stay away from fakers—I didn't have a clue. Who were these other men yapping with their mouths full, mustard on their lips, coleslaw on their teeth—gangsters and businessmen, kissing Nathan's ass. How did they get to be who they were?

"Hey kid, how are you?" Larry Spratz said to me as if we were old friends. He had a glass of champagne in his hand.

"Fine. Where's your brother?"

"He doesn't like parties. Looks like you got into another fight."

"Just fell into some garbage cans."

"A friend of yours is here, in the kitchen."

"Who?"

"Go surprise him."

Before I entered the kitchen I figured out who it must be. Morris was washing dishes and didn't see me till I came up beside him. Two of his fingers were now stubs but it looked like his hand still functioned. When he saw me he started crying and for a few seconds I wished I'd backed out of the kitchen before he noticed me. Maybe he was ashamed to be seen as Nathan's servant. But when he hugged me with his wet hands it felt good.

"Your father's here?"

"He's talking to some men. Should I get him?"

"No," Morris whispered, "When you're out of the building tell him that Rachel transferred to college in Canada so she's safe from him and I'll be sending you that postcard very soon."

"Israel?"

Morris open and shut his eyes three times.

Nathan banged on a glass with a knife to get everyone's attention.

There were about thirty men of different ages. Most looked like they were in their forties and fifties. Everyone stopped talking and crowded around Nathan who stood under an enormous crystal chandelier in the large dining room. I walked over to my father, who was standing alone.

Nathan hoisted his glass of champagne in the air. "Good Yontif."

"Good Yontif," many voices shouted back."

"Buona Fortuna," other voices shouted louder, as if competing.

Nathan took a sip and so did everyone else, including me. "First of all I want to thank everyone for coming." Nodding, he looked around at the people in the semicircle. He made eye contact with some and smiled at others. "Like all of you, I have things to atone for. Some of you, I know, think I have more than others." He chuckled. A few guests laughed nervously, glancing around. "A very close childhood friend of mine died a couple of months ago. I've been in mourning ever since. In our later years we grew apart."

"That might happen," I whispered to my father, "when you saw off your best friend's arm."

"If there's one lesson from this that I can pass on to you, it's forgive and forget. Don't let the years pass because of a feud. Life is too short." Nathan looked at my father and smiled. "L'chaim. Long Leben. Long life."

The guests all took another sip of champagne. I clinked glasses with my father and gulped down the rest of mine. He put his glass on the buffet table.

"Where's Pearl?" Nathan asked, walking toward us, his hand outstretched. "We have a date."

My father quickly drew the envelope, with a check inside, out of his pocket and slipped it into Nathan's hand. He didn't smile but I was positive that this graceful move gave him as much satisfaction as his most powerful home runs or greatest handball victories ever had. As a bonus he didn't have to shake that slimy palm.

"I never thought you would deliver the money," Nathan said, opening the envelope. "How did you do it?"

"Pearl and I pooled our resources."

Nathan put his hand on my father's shoulder. For a second a look of genuine sadness covered Nathan's face, and if I didn't despise him, I would have felt sorry for him. "I'm jealous. You've got Pearl. You're a lucky guy. When all these people leave, I'll be alone in my apartment."

"You won't be alone." The champagne bubbled in my brain. "You have all these dead ghosts."

As soon as I said the words I felt the awkwardness. I pointed to the mirrors, probably magnifying the faux pas but trying to work my way out of it. I saw Nathan's disdain for me reflected in triplicate.

"Whatever happened to that woman, Gloria, you were seeing?" My father asked, rescuing me.

"She wanted to mother me. Not what I'm looking for."

Nathan moved on to other guests and my father looked at me and said, "You're an idiot."

Bar Mitzvahs, New Years, days of atonement, some things never change. One of the gangsters, who my father knew from the handball courts years ago, started chatting with him and I wandered away. After the maid handed me a new glass of champagne I walked over to Larry, who sat by himself on a white sofa, looking lost without his twin. I plopped down beside him, spilling a little champagne on his pants, and asked how he got the X on his cheek. His face lit up like a little boy under a Christmas tree. He told me that it was a souvenir from the Korean War when he was ambushed in the latrine by six beefy rednecks and held down. They carved an X for "extermination," but reinforcements arrived—his brother—and together the twins pummeled the anti-Semites into bloody sausage. The Army discharged two of the soldiers with medical disabilities. Larry said there were no more anti-Semitic incidents during the Spratz brothers' service to their country.

I knew how cruel the brothers could be. I knew what they had done to my father. Still, listening to Larry reminisce, I felt some admiration. Maybe not my role model, yet in certain situations, like dealing with a Tony Goostaldi, he would be exactly the right man for the job.

I took another gulp of champagne, though I was already dizzy. Watching the guests and their reflections, I made up a game: Tough and Not So Tough. I got Larry to play with me. After placing all of the men at the party into one of the camps, I thought about other men I knew. Tony Goostaldi and Sam Spratz were Tough. Rabbi Skulnick and Cousin Joel were Not So Tough. Except for my father, all of the tough guys seemed to get what they wanted, regardless of how stupid they were. But that wasn't totally accurate because Tony didn't get Mara and when the party was over Nathan was going to be alone in his bed.

When I tried to rise my spinning head knocked me back onto the sofa.

I leaned against Larry. "Who's your role model?"
"What?"

"You know. Who do you look up to?"

"I don't know. Roosevelt. Einstein. Is that what you mean?"

"Yeah. Sort of. Anyone that you know personally?"

"Why do you want to know?"

He grasped my arm with his large hand. He bent over me; his head tilted, eyes glassy, and stopped his face only inches from mine. Up close, beside the X, there were pockmarks and scars and ruts. He breathed champagne on me. Maybe I shouldn't be asking him questions.

"Just curious."

"I'll tell you something, kid. I know what you're asking. I ain't never found no saints. You know what I'm saying?"

I nodded. His breath was suffocating.

"The best advice I can give you is you take a little from each guy. Your father's got some balls. Nathan's got brains. Your friend Morris he's a survivor. That tough guy over there he's a stand-up guy." He pointed to short wiry man in a black shirt and white sport jacket. "You know what I'm saying? You take a little. Up close, everyone's shit smells. You take a little of the good and you try it on. See if it fits."

He smiled, releasing my arm, which was now bruised, and sighed before leaning against the backrest. In less than a minute he was asleep. From across the room, my father waved that it was time to go. I stood up, trying to find some balance. I put my hand on Larry's shoulder and looked down at him. He was snoring, his arms folded protectively against his chest. Sleeping, he was Not So Tough.

# 24.

Two weeks after Yom Kippur, Grandma was released from the hospital. The doctors were surprised at how well she was doing. No one was talking about her dying anymore except for Grandma, who said that she was "fading."

A couple of afternoons later I met my father, mother, sister, and baby niece at Grandma's apartment. She was in her upholstered chair, too proud to lie in bed. Her head leaned way back on a yellow pillow that covered the tattered fabric.

Mr. Fein sat on an aluminum folding chair, his hands and head resting on his cane as his small brown eyes followed the conversation. His eyelids often closed for long intervals.

Suzy and I sat on Grandma's bed while our parents sat on the sagging couch. Marjorie slept on my mother's lap. She wore only a diaper, which needed changing. "Mom, our apartment in New Rochelle is beautiful," my mother said. "It will be ready in two weeks. Seven rooms. You can have your own bedroom.

We're on the water. Ducks and geese right outside your window. You have to come."

"I'm so weak, I can't move."

"Grandma, it's no good for you here," I said, glancing around the smelly room. The linoleum floor buckled from water damage caused by a leak in the steam pipes. Condensation slithered down the walls as cockroaches crawled up, so it looked like a highway with traffic going both ways.

"Ricky, you're a good boy. Listen to your Grandma. A person needs their own bed. Mr. Fein doesn't care. He leaves me during the day. I know he's no good, but this is my apartment. Thirty years."

"She's better off in her own house," my father said.

"What does she have here?" my mother asked.

"Him," Suzy said, pointing at Mr. Fein, who looked like he was asleep.

"You think I don't see? I'm a fool? I should have been a rabbi, everybody tells me. I know what a weasel he is. Twice a day he goes to the club, beautiful meals."

"Mrs. Simon," Mr. Fein said, his eyes still closed, his head shaking on the cane like a puppet on a stick, "it's not a club, it's a cafeteria."

"Quiet, you. He eats wonderful, comes home, doesn't want to eat. He starves me. So cheap. You think I don't know? He has no money for me, but he's a big sport with the other women at the club."

"Mrs. Simon." Mr. Fein laughed. He squeezed his closed eyes. "Vut vimin? Your grandmother thinks I fool around vith other vimim. It's not a club. I go there for some soup. Ten minutes. There's no vimin."

Grandma nodded her head, curling her lips bitterly. "We're sitting at the table, and I put my glass of water down in front of me." She became more animated, pantomiming the scene with her hands. "I turn around and the glass is on the other side of the table. I say, 'Mr. Fein, why you move my glass?' He says, 'Mrs. Simon, are you crazy, you put it down there.' He wants me to think I'm crazy. I know I put the glass here and he moves it there. This is what he did to his wife. A wonderful woman. He's the worst. The lowest. He wants my rent-controlled apartment, so he's conniving. But I'm old. Fershtay, my kinder? He gets my mail. I can't even light the stove anymore."

Grandma leaned back again, exhausted by her outburst. She fell asleep. Regardless of what the doctors said, she knew they were wrong. She was dying. It wasn't one thing. She had told me that her body felt weaker than she ever could remember. Her vision, already impaired, dimmed further. She could feel the pull of death, tugging at her. "I fight it, my kindalah," she'd said. "I fight it for you."

We all seemed to accept the day as lost, passing the afternoon in a steamy apartment watching an old woman sprawled on a ripped upholstered chair. Not my father though. He lacked the ability to adapt to his environment. He tried to impose his own rhythm on every situation and when he didn't succeed he became an outsider. He left the apartment to wait downstairs.

I studied my grandmother asleep, her glasses on her lap, her eyes glued together by a white paste she secreted. Her arms, only a few months ago big and fleshy and strong enough to carry two huge bundles of groceries, were now frail, the meat disappearing. I wondered if this decline would have happened even if I hadn't dropped the egg.

When Grandma woke up, she was groggy and far away. She groaned like a child awakened in the middle of the night. Lines by her eyes usually hidden by her glasses appeared red and deep as she nodded her head and scanned the room. She mumbled a few words to herself and nodded again.

"Ricky, are you still here?"

"Yes Grandma, I'm right here." I stroked her wrist.

"Ha ha, without glasses I don't see so well."

"You see everything," Suzy said. "You're so smart."

"So listen to me. You have a beautiful baby. Your husband's no prince, but he'll take care of you."

"He's cold Grandma, and selfish."

"You think he's perfect?" Grandma said, pointing at Mr. Fein, who laughed again. "You think your father doesn't have any faults?"

"I don't think he does," my mother said in a little girl's voice, talking to the baby.

"You have to move to New Rochelle," I said. "I'll starve without your good food."

"Move, shmove. Don't start in, you and your mother. What am I going to do there? You think it's easy to make new friends? If I was younger, maybe. You think it's so nice there? It's not so nice. My house looks swell, no?"

"Beautiful Grandma, just gorgeous."

She slapped my hand.

"We've got to go, Mom," my mother said, leaning over. "Susan has a train to catch. Think about coming."

"A person needs their own bed."

"So we'll move your bed," I said.

"Go. You're all crazy. Good luck in New Rochelle. Susan,

darling, God will be good to you and the baby for visiting me."

After Suzy changed the diaper, she held up Marjorie for Grandma to kiss.

I kissed my grandmother's cheek. "Get better quick."

"I will, my kutchymunion. Telephone me or write me a letter. Print big."

"I'll write you a letter on a napkin."

"God will be good to you, you hyenas."

Our family stepped into the dark hallway. Mr. Fein and Grandma sat alone on their chairs, their small hands waving, the steam pipes hissing, as we shouted goodbye.

"Ricky darling, come here." I rushed back. The smell like aged cheese engulfed me.

"Be good to your mother. Don't be like him. Don't hurt her."

"I'll be good, Grandma. Bye"

"You're a good boy."

"I'm a man now."

"Ha ha, you're a good boy, Rickalah. A good man."


My mother tried four more times to convince Grandma to move with us to New Rochelle, but she refused. Our new apartment was gorgeous. Three bedrooms and cross ventilation, the apartment extending from the front of the building to the back. Six stories below, ducks and geese played on the inlet that connected to Long Island Sound, which hooked up with the Atlantic Ocean, where my grandmother had crossed by ship as a child from Poland.

Now that we were out of the Bronx and exposed to a better

life and classier people, my mother said it was time for all of us to improve ourselves. She still worked for Arthur Posner but was planning on taking night school art classes again. She urged me to take French in school and read at least one book a week in addition to my homework. Suzy enrolled at the local community college to finish her degree in education (she and Marjorie had moved in with us when she left Jeffrey in October). Even my father stopped being a bookie and gave up smuggling tax-free cigarettes and all other illicit activities. Though he still snuck into movie theaters.

Salt air. Ducks on the water. This was where we belonged. The best family in the Bronx had moved up the ladder. It would be a long climb to become the best family in New Rochelle, but for the moment my mother's belief that she was an extraordinary person seemed to be validated. She had made it, out of the Bronx, and into a spacious apartment in Westchester County, one of the wealthiest areas in the country.

My new junior high school was only a block away from our building. It looked like a castle, set in the middle of large playing fields and surrounded by a wrought-iron fence. I didn't fit in at first. New Rochelle was not many miles from the Bronx, but the culture and people felt vastly different. Wealthier, better educated, better dressed, the kids just seemed more polished than me.

Missing my old neighborhood and old friends, I went back after six weeks and was shocked by how small and dirty the neighborhood looked. The wide sidewalks I remembered felt narrower and confined. The streets were full of litter, the people drained of energy. Saying hello to Fat Bertha and drinking a chocolate malted at Joe's was fun, but my friends seemed alien.

They looked at me like I was a snob and maybe I was becoming one. The kids in my new school seemed so much more attractive and appealing than these guys. My mother had always taught me that perspective was everything, and now that I was living in New Rochelle, the Bronx no longer cast its magic.

I knocked on Mara's door. When she opened it she smiled, but our conversation was awkward. We'd lost that old intimacy. Maybe now that she was a student at Walton High School, she didn't have time anymore for an eighth grader or maybe moving to the suburbs had already changed me. We kissed goodbye and promised to stay in touch, but I think we both knew we weren't going to.

By the time I left the neighborhood, I was never coming back. I might not be truly at home yet in New Rochelle but that was the world I was looking to conquer. With no real new friends I spent a lot of time playing by myself or helping my sister with the baby. After school I sometimes ran around the field at my junior high, nursing a fantasy of qualifying for the Olympics. One day some neighborhood kids who so far had ignored me, were playing touch football and needed another player. One of them shouted to me as I ran, "Hey, track star, you want to play?"

"Sure," I said, and that was it. I was now part of a new neighborhood.

Of course this New Rochelle life could fall apart quickly. Tax season was approaching and Elizabeth Taylor's accountants would soon be looking at her bank account. My mother still owed several thousand dollars to assorted friends. Our rent in New Rochelle was $220 a month instead of $70. So much of our future depended on the settlement. The supermarket's insurance company was in no rush to pay. My mother would have to find money somewhere to put back into Elizabeth Taylor's account before the accountants discovered the shortfall. She could play a shell game and move money out of Marilyn Monroe's account and into Elizabeth's and then replenish Marilyn's with money from Tennessee Williams and keep moving the money ahead of the accountants. The timing would have to be perfect. Not the best idea. Marilyn's account was shrinking. Tennessee watched his money.

"Would you borrow from Nathan again?" I asked her when she was short the second month's rent.

"Never!"

"Good. How you going to..."

"Friends will come through."

If Grandma's sacrifice paid off, and we got a big settlement, it would become family lore that she was the one who saved us from Nathan and delivered us out of the Bronx. She would be the horse we rode to the winner's circle. Not Dream Away Lodge. Not the sure thing. Not the quick fix. Grandma, who endured, who was in it for the long haul, would be the *dark horse* that my father had prophesied would save the day.

# 25.

When Mr. Fein called, in November, to tell us that Grandma had died, my mother, Suzy, and I were playing Scrabble. Though her death wasn't totally unexpected, my mother was inconsolable at first. She held the receiver of the phone as if handing it to one of us, shook her head back and forth, and tears started streaming down her cheeks. Then the wailing began. My sister and I started wailing as well. This woke up Marjorie, who must have been shocked that anyone but her could cry so loudly. As if it was a competition, she joined in.

"She should have come live with us," my mother moaned.

"She didn't want to," I said.

"We should've tried harder."

"We did," I said, hugging her. "She died the way she wanted to, in her own apartment, in her own bed."

The funeral was small. She had outlived most of her friends.

A few poker players came, Clara, a couple of neighbors, Cousin Harvey, Cousin Freddy, Cousin Eva in a wheelchair. My mother, Suzy, and I wept. Mr. Fein didn't shed a tear. Nor did my father, who sat several feet away from the rest of our family.

After the service, which lasted less than half an hour, my mother, father, Suzy, Marjorie, and I took the subway to Grand Central Station, where we would catch a train to New Rochelle. Like the Huguenots escaping persecution in La Rochelle, France, and starting over across the sea, the Davis family was beginning anew.

"I'm alone," my mother said as we sat in the first subway car. Suzy gave Marjorie a bottle in the corner seat. My father slept, his head bobbing. "I don't know what's going to happen."

I squeezed her hand. "Grandma will look out for us."

She nodded. That Grandma was watching over us seemed to help her with her grief. Her mother had been so entwined with her own adult life that her absence left a huge void.

For me too. She had always been there to take care of me. I wanted to believe that she somehow would still look out for us, make the settlement happen, and let us stay in New Rochelle. The train rattled. Lights flickered. "A mother knows," my mother said through her sobs. "Only a mother knows. You give so much for your children. Family is everything. Remember that, Ricky."

Daddy said sex is everything, I almost blurted out. Instead, I said nothing, letting her grieve. Her body shook as the train rocked. She had hardly stopped crying since hearing of her mother's death. I felt anxious and stood up and went over to the front of the car, watching the light pass through dark, the belly, the ugly soot caked along the tunnel, the steel rails guiding us, and I could feel the grief coursing through my mother's body. She sobbed louder and I looked back at her. She stared at me with such sadness. I felt her pull, wanting me to return to comfort her. I turned back to the tunnel and looked ahead, watching the yellow light lead the way—my face pressed against the door, squashing my nose and lips as my breath condensed on the wired glass. I fought back the tears. I imagined playing tag. I was running, trying to get to the safety zone and touch the pole or box or tree that had been designated safe from the tagger, that haven where a child was immune from the powers of the *It*.

A train raced alongside ours, traveling a fraction faster, the sound of both trains rumbling within a couple of feet of each other. I stared through the side window at the men and women on that train, so close, caught in time, reading newspapers, sleeping, frozen for an instant. As if we were in different dimensions we saw each other intimately for a second in the yellow light, but in another second we would pass on never to touch again.

I waved to a pretty young woman sitting alone, a paperback open on her lap. She saw that I was waving and laughed. Her train pulled ahead and I waved again, reaching out for her. She pressed her hand to her lips and blew me a kiss.

My train slowed to a stop at another station, picking up people crowding the platform. I saw faces: Irish, Hispanic, Jewish, Asian, black, and fingers pulling out a chocolate bar from a candy machine, and sexy lips chewing gum in a broken mirror.

The train lurched forward again, picking up speed. My heart started to race. My mother cried. I felt the vibrations of the train shake throughout my body. The rumble of engines on the move. I smiled at my mother, though she wasn't looking at me now. Just watching her sitting there, crying, talking to herself, eased my anxiety about the future. She would sacrifice like her mother. Do whatever it took to save her family and figure out a way to make it work. She always did.

The light of a new station came into view. I felt filled with sadness but also hope, out of sorts but optimistic. Inside my head I began to chant the mantra from Hide and Seek, one I had shouted hundreds of times on warm summer nights: "Ready or not, here I come."

# Acknowledgements

Yikes. So much help. So many people. The act of writing might be solitary, but finishing a novel is, at least for me, a collective enterprise. I first started writing this novel forty years ago. In the early days, I was encouraged by fellow writers, James Leo Herlihy, James Kirkwood, and Francine Prose, as well as the supportive literary agents, Jay Garon and Dick Duane, and the editors, Tom Davis and Juri Jurevicks. My best friend, Michael Rosenfeld, was an early reader and fan. And has stayed with me throughout.

For years, when I was raising my family, I didn't write but when I began again I was lucky to play basketball with the *Atlantic Monthly* editor, C. Michael Curtis, whose writing advice was very helpful. He also put me in touch with Cynthia Vann who edited a different novel that I was writing, but taught me a lot. Cheeni Rai and the Iowa Book Doctors also edited mainly my other novel, *The Struggle to be Good*, but I learned so much from them.

Trish Perry, Beth Rosen, Larry Kellam, Rob Wyman, Barbara Lucey, Naomi Rosenfeld, Michael Knoedler, Dawn Carroll, Joan and Peter Cocks, and Amir Soltani graciously took the time to read early drafts. So did Kathy Dwyer and Vinnie Chase. Lila Naimark read several versions and offered great suggestions. I am forever grateful to my chosen test readers, Rick Gordon, Ed Englander, Sherry Payne, Kathy Reticker, Roxanne Wariners, Naomi Rosenfeld, Alan Shapiro, Chris Perry, Sharon Bially, Marlene Dodes-Callahan, Elise Ritvo Kaufman, and the lady from Long Island I met at the Harvard Book Store whose name I misplaced.

Finding Grub Street, a wonderful, supportive literary community in Boston, was a writing bonanza for me. I apologize if I can't remember all my classmates for they all offered good advice. Some of them are Leslie Greffenius, Dell Smith, Louis Panatagopulous, Ann Killough, Mary Burket, Kimberley Morrisette, Nichole Bernier, Julie Wu, Miriam Sidanius, Amin Ahmad, and Pat Gillen.

I particularly want to thank Henriette Power, Randy Susan Meyers, and Pauline Chen for taking the time, outside of class, to read a whole draft and offer great advice. Gregory Maguire was also generous enough to read a draft and make suggestions.

There is also the administrative staff of Grub Street, who are remarkable. Eve Bridburg, Christopher Castellani, Whitney Scharer, and my fellow badger, Sonya Larson. Then there are the Grub teachers and editors who gave me some polish. Lisa Borders helped with *The Struggle to be Good*. Sophie Powell and Stuart Horwitz offered me excellent critical advice and their positive feedback gave me the confidence to continue. Dawn Dorland wasn't an instructor at Grub Street but a young classmate and gifted writer, who has become my friend. She is also an amazing editor whose advice I rely on. And of course there is Jenna Blum, best selling author, wonderful teacher, fabulous editor, and friend, who revived me as a writer.

Even with all this help I still needed more and I am thankful to the professional editors, Benee Knauer and Nancy

Doherty, for their support and editing insights (Nancy was also my eighth grade prom date). My old high school friend, Ken Davis, made some good suggestions. Jane Roper wrote the blurb copy for the back cover. My copy editor, Eileen Kramer, was great to work with. The literary agent, Susan Finesman, was very supportive. Ladette Randolph was kind enough to read my novel and write a blurb. Randall Warniers designed layouts of the draft books for my test readers. Michelle Toth published the *The Bookie's Son* and gave me both writing and publishing advice.

I especially want to thank my son Max who designed the cover and layout, my daughter Lucy who did the illustrations, and Pat, my wife of forty-two years, who had to put up with my need to write. To all of my team, for whatever good is in this book, I am eternally grateful.

Made in the USA
Lexington, KY
25 May 2012